NIGHTFALL

BENSON FIRST RESPONDERS
BOOK 6

LISA PHILLIPS

eBook ISBN: 979-8-88552-188-8

Paperback ISBN: 979-8-88552-189-5

Published by Two Dogs Publishing, LLC. Idaho, USA

Cover Design by Sasha Almazan and Gene Mollica, GS Cover Design Studio, LLC

Edited by Christy Callahan, Professional Publishing Services

Audiobook published by Recorded Books

ONE

"Three minutes."

Jamal twisted around to face Malik. "That's all? We have to get out of the blast radius."

Daniel shoved them both aside and flipped the locks on the crate. He lifted the lid and revealed the bomb they'd packed carefully inside before they carried it into this container ship.

Jamal looked at his father's watch on his wrist—the one his grandfather had worn in France in the fall of forty-four. The one Jamal's father wore in Korea when he was barely out of high school. Jamal had both lost and found it during Desert Storm. He'd had it repaired, and the thing kept ticking—like the beat of his heart, a relentless thump that reminded him with each marked moment to leave a legacy in this world.

Daniel flicked the switch on the bomb. The timer began its countdown, its legacy in the world.

Jamal said, "For our children and the world they will live in."

Daniel stood. "For the earth and all who come after us."

Malik held the flip phone in his hand, tapping it against his other palm as though nervous for this device he had assembled. Trained by the Army to disarm bombs. Now he put that skill to good use. "For those who shroud us in darkness, so that they will pull back the veil and show us the truth."

Jamal stared at the timer, the span of a few seconds counting down. "Let's get out of here. Or we'll go down as martyrs to our own cause."

He headed for the door of this lower deck storage room and drew his pistol. A thud behind him caught his attention. He turned in time to see Daniel standing over Malik, who had collapsed to his knees and was grasping his head.

Jamal gasped. They needed to get out of here, and they were fighting? "What are you—"

Daniel fired his gun. Malik dove to the side but caught the bullet anyway and hit the floor beside the bomb crate. Then Daniel turned to Jamal.

He fled through the door to the hall.

The narrow hall with metal walls on either side. It smelled like rust and decades of ocean spray that had come running down the stairs from the decks above.

A kill box. Daniel had funneled them into a spot where they had little chance to get away.

Jamal reached the stairs, swung back around with his back to the wall, and fired two shots at his friend. A shot pinged off the wall beside Jamal's face. Daniel ducked back into the room.

"You'll die down here!" Jamal would ensure this betrayal

went no farther. He scrambled up the stairs to the door at the front and shoved it open.

Two sailors with grimy clothes and their white faces weathered by the sea. They weren't supposed to be here. Both wore ragged beanies and beards that touched their shirtfronts. "Hey!"

Jamal raced the other way, even though it took him deeper into the ship. He needed to get out of here.

They chased him, both men pounding the floor under them. Relentlessly pursuing him down the hall. He shoved through a hatch into another room and raced through it.

Gunshots exploded behind him, back down the hall. Daniel had found the men? Had he killed again? Their statement wasn't supposed to have life-ending consequences. It was purely political. A way to make the government take notice of them.

Now one man was already dead.

Would Daniel blame the whole thing on them, leaving them too dead to defend themselves? Had his plan all along been to kill them and escape during the confusion?

Jamal's gut twisted the way it had when he held his son in his arms for the first time and realized he would never be the man Blake needed him to be.

He found another door and shoved it open. Metal hit metal, and he raced up the stairs, stumbling as he went. His shin hit the edge of a step. Jamal cried out the pain and frustration, louder than he needed to. It was all going wrong.

Daniel had double-crossed them.

Malik, whom they'd sweat and bled with in Iraq, was dead. As if their bond of friendship as brothers-in-arms meant nothing to Daniel.

Jamal shoved out onto the deck under a canopy of dark

clouds. Coastal wind whipped at his collar. He ducked his head and ran down the starboard side.

Someone yelled behind him. Those men? Daniel?

Jamal didn't look back. He levered his body over the side and into the black water.

The splash took his breath away. Jamal descended beneath the surface and stared up but could see nothing through the murky water.

Then, an orange ball.

The concussive force of the explosion heaved through the water, shoving him back. He collided with something under the surface and swallowed lungfuls of water. His chest burned. Jamal kicked up to the surface. Pain rippled through his back. He breached and sucked in air, the strength leaving his limbs. The shipping container had split almost in half, now descending beneath the surface on fire.

Sirens blared in the distance.

Someone cried and called out for help. Jamal beat back the water to turn. He could swim out into the ocean, descend beneath the surface when he ran out of power, and leave his story untold—or he could escape. Abandon the plan that was supposed to happen when they fled. Before the explosion.

It was over now.

The ship erupted with another blast.

Water swelled, shoving him back against something again. Jamal's head cracked into a solid object, a post or another boat, and everything went black.

It was over.

SOMETIME LATER, HE REGAINED AWARENESS TO FIND himself lying in a bed. Covered with sheets and a blanket.

Pain in his elbow—a needle—and his head. Jamal lifted his hand to touch his head, but his hand snagged.

He blinked and managed to focus on his wrist. Cuffed to a hospital bed.

His friends were dead. His chance at a legacy was over.

He'd been arrested.

TWO

Detective Blake Reed pushed open the doors to the Intelligence division. In a smaller city like Benson, this division acted more like major crimes wrapped up in intelligence gathering, focusing on a broader view of crime in the city rather than arresting one bad guy at a time.

The sergeant's door was open.

Blake's phone buzzed in his pocket, but he ignored it. His sisters had been blowing up their group chat all morning about one of Mercy's professors, then it was about what Grace had for breakfast, and finally, what Destiny was doing today in Africa. She hadn't yet replied this morning about how her mission trip was going.

Four desks in the main room, and none were occupied.

He glanced at the board on the way down the hall to the bullpen. Officer Jesse and Detective Caurelle were out currently, which meant they'd shown up for shift this morning and were already on the streets.

The fourth cop in Intelligence was Detective Wilks, six months from retirement—a "house mouse" just doing paperwork and biding his time until he could punch the clock that final time and get to his houseboat permanently instead of just on the weekend.

Wilks wasn't in yet, unsurprising since it wasn't quite eight in the morning. The guy never came in before nine. More than once, Blake had caught him tipping the contents of a flask into his coffee.

Blake dumped his backpack under his desk and fired up his computer but didn't sit. A new case had been tacked up on the board—overnight or early this morning. He walked over to the wall of corkboards. Two cases in the last month had become three.

Each victim was a local and a known dealer. The most recent was Carl Cleary, twenty-six. A few years younger than Blake. Like the others, he was a person of interest in drug-related crime over the past few months, and similarly, Carl was first stabbed and then shot in the head. A curious manner of death that no one on the streets wanted to talk about.

"Reed."

He turned to find the sergeant at the door to her office. Sergeant Megan Deerdan was in her fifties with two college-age sons and a divorce under her belt. She wore low heels and a skirt suit that held her tight enough that it seemed scared to do anything but submit. She had her jacket buttoned and her hair straightened to within an inch of its life. Barely any makeup, though she didn't much need it.

The woman lived on coffee, arrests, and six-inch meatball subs.

Decades ago, she'd busted a huge ring of weapons smugglers from Alaska, and the same year, she won the Washington State police boxing championship—women's division. She still fought. She still worked out every day. And she didn't seem to have slowed down at all.

"Sergeant." Blake nodded. "I was catching up on the new case."

"Good." Sergeant Deerdan stepped out with an empty coffee mug in one hand and her phone in the other. "Jesse and Caurelle are with the medical examiner trying to get evidence that we can match to a murder weapon."

"That would be good." All they'd been able to ascertain so far was that the victims had been killed with the same gun. "Anything you want me to focus on this morning?"

The sergeant nodded. "You need to look into the center angle." She moved to the board and tapped a paper on the second case, then ran her finger to the third. "Both of the victims in these cases had connections to the Benson Fresh Start Center for Teens. I'd like you to pay them a visit, look around, and find out if there's any connection."

"You mean, if the center is tied to the drug deals they had going on?"

Deerdan said, "They were either rivals or they ignored each other's existence."

Blake's phone buzzed in his pocket again, then again twice in quick succession. He lifted his wrist and watched the notifications flash up. They were talking about chip flavors. "Far as I know, they worked in opposite areas around Benson. Different territories. Different supplier. Just like the first two murders."

"Whatever is going on, we need to put a stop to it before we have a parade of bodies and we run out of wall space." Deerdan walked over to the new case. "Cleary was killed after midnight Sunday, so the leads are fresh."

"Homicide passed it over? I thought this guy died last night."

Deerdan shook her head. "They had it for eighteen hours and then sent it when it popped up as connected."

Blake knew the homicide detectives who worked downstairs, including Westbrook and Hummet. They hadn't had an open spot when he'd forgone the sergeant's exam and decided to go for detective instead. Intelligence had the fifth floor, under the admin offices and the commissioner's office upstairs. On the ground floor were the public facing areas and the Benson FBI office—a tiny satellite department crammed into one room.

"Take a look at the center angle. Let me know what pops."

"Copy that, Sergeant." Blake got a cup of coffee and downloaded the file to his computer.

Detective Wilks trudged in a short time later, smelling like cigars.

Blake scrolled on his mouse wheel. "Good morning."

"Is it?" Wilks sank into his chair, groaning like an old dog. "Hadn't noticed."

Blake's phone vibrated across the top of the desk. Jasper's name flashed on the screen. He lifted it and answered, "Reed."

"Catch a case this morning?"

"You hear anything about the teen center being involved?"

Jasper paused a beat, then put on an accent. "The center ain't exactly white collar."

Sounded like his friend would rather be looking into Blake's case than his own. Did he hate the department he'd been sent to as well? "Where you're at isn't so bad, is it?"

Jasper completely ignored that. "Isn't that center where

your sisters used to go after school, 'cause they had that program, and you had class or work?"

"Yep." Blake's four sisters had passed through those doors hundreds of times over a period of a few years.

"So ask them if they think there's drugs moving through."

"Is that why you called?" Blake pushed his chair back and took his mug to the break room they shared with the rest of the floor.

Jasper said, "Nope."

Two officers sat at a table eating breakfast and shooting the breeze, though both looked like they'd had a rough night. He lifted his chin and went to the coffeepot. Their one-word answers were a language of its own. SWAT had worked together so long the guys felt like brothers. But the department disbanded the family to a part-time detail—which he and Jasper were still on.

Gage was a lieutenant and worked on a different floor, on different shifts. Blake hadn't seen him in weeks.

Liam had married Roxie over Thanksgiving, and they were now training with the Northwest Counter-Terrorism Taskforce somewhere down in Oregon.

Jasper worked in white-collar crimes and refused to talk about whether he liked it or not. "Have you talked Destiny into coming home from Africa yet?"

Blake wasn't sure he wanted to force her to change her plans. He'd never been that kind of brother, even if he'd practically raised the girls. "Last I checked, she's a grown woman who makes her own choices."

"It's dangerous. She could get killed."

"You don't think the organization she's going with has figured out how to keep their volunteers alive?"

Jasper let out a frustrated sound.

Blake knew that pain. With four younger sisters, he'd

spent half his life with sleepless nights, worrying about where they were and who might be hurting them. Or running background checks on their boyfriends. This wasn't the time to get into why Destiny's whereabouts might be Jasper's business. "She gets to choose for herself. She's an adult." After a beat, he asked, "Anything else?"

"You're not gonna like it."

"No kidding." Hence, the beating around the bush. "What's going on?"

"My lieutenant found a connection on my case to a guy busted for fraud a few years back. They want your old man to make an approach, see if he's amenable to giving us intel."

"Because your lieutenant can't drive out to the prison and ask for himself?" Whether he asked Blake's dad or the other man didn't matter. At least Blake wouldn't be in the middle of it.

"I'll ask the warden to talk to your dad. Or the guy connected to our suspect. I just wanted to run it by you first."

Blake squeezed the mug so hard it was in danger of cracking in his hand. Just as long as the girls didn't find out he'd been there. "I'll get word to have him call me. Send me the information."

"You're the best, B."

"Yeah, yeah." They were both detectives now. SWAT brothers as different as two men could be—Jasper, the son of a state senator, and Blake, the son of a man who'd killed and maimed his victims.

At least according to his criminal record.

Only God—if He was even real—knew who the killer in the family was.

THREE

Violet stood in the center of the room, hands out, fingers splayed. The Center was the place where mistakes became dreams and brokenness was forged into the promise that life could get better. She lifted her chin. "Put the gun down, Drew."

The two teens squared off against each other beside the chessboard, the pieces made of things they'd found at an electronics recycle store. Pieces they'd fashioned themselves.

If they knocked that board over, or jostled the pieces, two others—preteen boys—would be upset. "We can talk about this, Drew. But I need you to put down that gun."

He looked more nervous than Austin, who had the gun pointed at him.

All bravado, but the fear was buried just underneath because he refused to show the world how he felt about anything. Austin would much rather be the tough guy.

Drew shifted his weight from one foot to the other, the gun shaky in his hand. "He stole from me. He ripped me off and kept my money."

Austin just stared.

Both were seventeen, and about to age out of foster care. Barely still in high school. Dropped out of high school. The kind of older boys who believed they were men, role models for the preteens with their weeks-long chess match. Hardly a good example.

Pretty much her life as well.

Nothing anyone would use as a shining example of how to succeed in the world. Her life had crashed and burned to epic proportions. At least she had a job, a mission, and the love of a good God who hadn't let her go. Right now nothing else mattered—except these kids.

Austin and Drew both needed to discover what she knew about the center. Namely, that it was the difference between hope and despair. The kids who got it discovered a purpose. They went on from here to live their lives, emailing on occasion to tell her what they were up to. Maybe it wasn't Harvard Law School in a lot of cases, but it also wasn't jail or the kind of rock bottom she'd lived.

The ones that didn't? Kids like Austin, who pushed back at every turn until she didn't know why he came around—except to make deals. The ones that kept her awake at night and grieved her heart, knowing they had chosen destruction in the name of freedom.

Drew was one who could make it...hopefully.

But not if he had a gun.

Violet took another step across the expansive common area. Pool tables at one end. Couches and an aging game console that liked to overheat in the middle of a level. Tables where kids did homework after school. The door opposite her led to the basketball courts, then the parking lot, where snow covered the ground. The kids had started a fire in the huge fireplace. She didn't ask where they got the wood from.

"Drew, we've got a couple of options here." Violet kept

her voice steady. "We can figure this out as a group." He didn't need to take this on himself. It was part of why he was here, because they considered themselves a team—a family. So many of these kids had poor excuses for family.

Which only made her think of her dad, but that was a whole different mountain to climb.

"We can sit for a tribunal."

"Or you can put that gun down, kid." The low male voice thundered through the room. No excuses, no nonsense.

Both boys flinched. Violet probably did too, but she was more focused on them. "He is right." She needed to soften the situation, not shove Drew's back to the wall and give him no choice but to surrender—something no man, let alone a teen boy, wanted to do. "So, let's do a tribunal, and we can figure this out."

He didn't have to go it alone.

That's what the center stood for. It was the reason Violet showed up here to volunteer every chance she got when she wasn't working.

Because she needed it as much as the kids did.

You aren't alone.

God had been there for her. In the aftermath of that fallout, where everything she'd worked for had come crashing down, He had still been there. *Thank You, Lord.*

She needed the words to say now. The wisdom to know how to handle this.

"Tribunal." Drew spat the word out. His strength faltered, and the gun dipped.

The man who'd practically yelled across the room strode in front of her, and she blinked at the width of his shoulders. But only because she was used to dealing with teens who were far less...man than this guy.

Austin shifted back and started to turn.

"Sit down," she said.

He rolled his eyes and slumped onto the back of the couch, folding his arms.

She wasn't going to turn him over to the police. As if they'd figure out what had happened between Drew and Austin. They'd only find something to charge both kids with and probably try them as adults. She wouldn't wish prison on anyone. Especially not almost-adults, who would get eaten alive when faced with real criminals.

Mr. Man Dude had Drew's gun, and he wasn't a cop because he hadn't cuffed Drew or thrown him to the ground. She walked to the wall and hit the button for the intercom they'd had installed for announcements. "Tribunal. Ten minutes."

She walked back to Drew and the man, who was now holding the gun in one hand. She unfolded a paper bag from the craft drawer with a quick flick of her wrists. "In here." The guy stared at her with huge brown eyes she wanted to stare at for hours.

Nope.

Too bad he was good-looking. Like stop traffic good-looking. *Too bad.* More like epically tragic. This was probably the worst time in her life to meet someone she could actually be attracted to.

"I'm Lettie." She held up the bag. "Drop the gun in. I'll take it to the amnesty bin."

She could do it on her way to work tonight since she was on a night shift. It wouldn't be much out of her way to stop at the police station near work and drop it in the weapons surrender bin, where anyone could leave a knife, gun, or any other deadly weapon with no questions asked. It was a successful way to get illegal and legal weapons off the streets.

And exactly where she was going to put this gun.

He clicked something on the gun, and the magazine fell out of the bottom. He slid the top back, and Drew caught the bullet that flew out. This guy knew how to disarm a weapon? Oh, that was helpful. She knew basically nothing about guns. Big surprise. Her dad only hunted caviar and cigars so he could have a night in with fifty of his closest friends and waiters serving crab cakes.

Violet rolled the top of the bag over. "Drew, you want to help me set up for the meeting?"

He nodded, his expression still tense.

She fought back the need to ask him questions about what'd happened. But the opportunity to allow kids who had no autonomy in the world the chance for justice beat out her curiosity. She got to give them the gift of being able to use reason and logic, to make a decision about the consequences of a wrong done and see the process through to satisfaction.

And Austin knew it was better than her calling the police. His oldest brother was doing a stretch in the local county jail that would last until Austin was nearly thirty.

She got to offer them the chance to decide their fate for themselves and a shot at justice in a world that rarely gave them either.

And for her, it was a moment where she didn't have to think about the giant *F* on her forehead. The one that stood for "failure" and encapsulated what she'd done and who she was.

She needed this place of second chances as much as the kids did.

Mr. Good-Looking had a situational awareness she saw in kids who lived on the streets. A need to clock the exits and keep the threat in view. Still, when he stepped forward and held out his hand, his eyes were soft. "I'm Blake. You're really Lettie?"

"What does that mean?" She shook his hand, amused enough by his reaction to her that she found herself laughing. That hadn't happened in a while.

He grinned and gave her hand one last squeeze. Like he didn't want to let go.

"I have to get ready for the tribunal." Not get distracted by a *man*. "Nice to meet you."

The last thing she needed was a wild card tossed in the middle of her deck.

FOUR

She walked away, and Blake caught the kid staring at him. Not good. He didn't need a teen boy about to face a tribunal—whatever that was—realizing that he recognized her name.

Lettie.

This was her.

He'd known there was a chance he would run into her. His sisters barely stopped talking about the amazing Lettie at the center and how great she was.

This woman? Not exactly what he'd pictured. After all, she was knock-him-flat gorgeous, and his sisters had never once offered to set him up with their hero. Their favorite adult. He had to admit, that was a little worrisome.

Either there was something they knew about Lettie that meant he wasn't a good candidate for her...or they believed he wasn't good enough for her. So was it that she didn't like cops, or something else? Or was it that he didn't measure up?

He wasn't sure which he'd root for.

Either way, it left him with the reality that he was a cop and it was all he'd ever be. The work he did as a police officer had value in the world. If he wasn't going to have a relationship, then fine. Why bother worrying about it?

He glanced over at the kid whose statement he should be taking, if he had been wearing his badge and holding a notebook. "So, what's this tribunal thing?"

The kid studied him like a guy who'd seen enough that he was jaded. Not surprising since he'd stared down the barrel of a gun and barely flinched.

If he could get the kid's last name from his ID, then Blake would run him for priors. If he had to peg someone as being connected to illegal dealings coming out of the center, this guy would be top of the list. But he couldn't move on a hunch—or even a gut feeling. He needed probable cause to get a warrant, and then he could look into the kid's background and figure this out.

Finally, the kid shrugged a shoulder. "Dumb. But it gets her off my back."

"What about Drew? He seemed pretty sure you stole from him. Enough to bring a gun and shove it in your face." Blake had heard enough of the conversation to know this was Austin.

"Not the first time." The kid sniffed. "Doubt it will be the last."

"And the money?"

"How'd you know it was money?"

So, the kid didn't know he'd been listening to pretty much the whole conversation. From the moment Lettie had stepped between the two teens and put herself in the line of fire to talk the armed one down. Given all the stories his sisters had told him about the woman, she'd been volunteering here for several years. Long enough that both Mercy and Hope knew her.

Destiny and Grace were older, though Grace and Mercy

were closest in age. Hope was about to graduate high school in the summer. Just a few months left and his youngest sister would be out in the world.

There would never be a time in his life when the sleepless nights of worry for his girls would be over.

Destiny was currently off doing whatever it was in Africa. He'd known the server job at Backdraft in Benson wouldn't last forever, but he'd never figured she would choose that long term. Not with the way she and Jasper looked at each other.

Mercy and Grace were both in college locally. They came over on Sundays after they went to church and forced him to eat charcuterie and watch whatever movie they'd chosen.

Hope worked at a bakery in Benson one night after school and Saturdays. After church, she did a lot of homework. However, she came over on occasion.

Blake had heard about Lettie from his three younger sisters. Enough that he felt like he knew her. But getting to see that woman hold out her hands and talk down a teenager, resolving what could've been a deadly situation? She was nothing like what they'd said.

And everything in him wanted to know her.

Too bad it wasn't meant to be.

Blake looked at the table setup Lettie and Drew were working on, joined by half a dozen kids who'd shown up after her intercom call. They all seemed to know what this was. Some kind of grand jury type hearing?

"You think she'd mind if I took a look around?" Did he need to give Austin the spiel about him being a security expert here to provide the center with a free consult? "Get a feel for what y'all do here?"

"Suit yourself." Another shoulder shrug.

Blake kept a leisurely pace as he headed out of the common area. He needed to come back with more than a hunch about some of the kids. He should grab the gun she'd bagged and take it with him, but if he told her why, she'd know who he was. He'd rather keep a low profile in a place like this where there wasn't a lot of trust for law enforcement.

He'd make better inroads if he stayed undercover.

And if Lettie were the kind of woman who relied on and trusted cops, she'd have called 911 first rather than stepping into that situation herself.

She knew what she was doing. He even respected her for it—if she could manage to do it without getting herself killed.

He found two guys, midtwenties each, on the basketball court. The ball bounced off the backboard and came his way. Blake wandered onto the court, even though he had jeans on with his tennis shoes, and tossed it back. "Hey."

The guy caught the ball and lifted his chin.

"I usually play over at the courts on Menchen, but this is a pretty sweet setup." He glanced around, eyeing the blackboard that looked to be used as a scoreboard. The walls were breeze-block, the lower half covered with padding like a crash mat. Parts of the padding were dented or torn. "I'm Blake."

"Hound." The guy motioned to his friend. "Pat."

Blake lifted his chin in return. Hound passed the ball back to him, and Blake tossed it at the basket. Pretty risky shot since he was farther away than normal. But it sank into the basket, and he didn't let on how surprised he was. Pat caught the ball after it bounced, and the two men came over.

"You guys hang out here?"

Hound sauntered, the swagger of a guy who'd made enough money it crept into the way he walked. The guy sniffed and shot him a look. "Lookin' for new turf?"

Blake said, "Scoping out security for my company. But that ain't what I make money at. Remote door locks pay out one time, and then there's all the maintenance. Easier to sell candy."

Hound and Pat glanced at each other.

"But if this is your store, I'll back off." He lifted both hands. "I'm not interested in fuss, even if it'd be worth it to stick around and visit with Lettie." Blake put an appropriate amount of male interest into his tone.

Hound snorted. "She ain't gonna give you nothin'."

'Cause he'd already tried? Blake asked, "What about that tribunal? Seems like serious business?"

"Kids playing grand jury." Pat snorted.

"How long you guys been hanging around here?" Blake needed a way to get their photos. Did Lettie have surveillance cameras in this place? If he couldn't run their IDs, he'd settle for following them when they left here to see where they lived or worked.

Hound shrugged. "Since we were kids, I guess."

"Now you operate out of the center?"

Pat took a step toward him that could be catalogued as aggressive but was more likely the man making a statement. "We don't need another business partner if that's what you're wondering. So stick to cameras, yeah?"

Blake nodded. "Got it."

He wasn't going to get in on their business, unless that was the way his sergeant wanted him to do this. He could create a vacuum and walk into it if he needed that inroad. Otherwise, he'd stick to information gathering and work up enough on these guys to dig into their lives—with a warrant.

"I'm gonna go back to my *surveillance* in the common room." He stepped back and lifted his brows. "She's in there, right?"

Both the men chuckled. Hound said, "Yeah, good luck with that, brother."

Blake flicked two fingers and did a circuit of the building's hallways, getting the layout locked in his mind just in case. He heard her before she came into view.

He leaned against the doorframe and watched, seriously appreciating the view. She commanded the room. All the kids were engaged, whether they were the subject or a member of the cohort who would pass judgment.

Yeah, this could get dangerous in a number of ways. Hopefully, he could keep her safe.

Even if it was from him.

FIVE

"Austin?" Violet glanced over at him, sitting at a table to the side facing the middle of the room. Drew sat on the other side, and the kids were all lined up in front of her so that they made the four sides of a square. Everyone equal.

Now, they knew Austin had two grand worth of Drew's... something. Money, drugs, some other stuff maybe. They wouldn't say. But even a few hundred would've been a lot. Once, they'd done a tribunal over a soda from the vending machine because Violet wasn't about to trivialize anyone's sense of injustice. Not when teenage feelings were so tenuous.

They needed to feel as though they were heard and treated fairly.

"Fine." Austin's mouth flattened into a line. "I'll provide *compensation* right now on Venmo." He lifted his phone off the table in front of him and tapped the screen.

Everyone waited.

The cohort of kids who'd listened to both sides of the story sat watching, mostly listening. A couple were on their phones, but that didn't mean they weren't aware of what was going on. She'd learned that one soon after she started here.

Violet looked at the accuser.

Drew's phone chimed. He looked at the screen. "Got it." Relief washed over his face. "I'm saving for a car. I need the money."

He'd told them that Austin promised to double what he had, but when Drew changed his mind, the other teen didn't want to let him back out of the deal. It had been a bad idea from the start. Far too risky.

"What are you saving for?"

Drew said, "I'm gonna buy a car. Get my GED and get out of here."

He wanted freedom. Most likely, that meant escaping his mom, who had good and bad days. Not many of the kids talked about their parents. Occasionally, social workers dropped by to see them. Drew's mom had stumbled in one evening when he'd been in the middle of a first-person shooter game tournament. She'd been blind drunk and covered in scratches.

"Considering others isn't real popular these days." Violet surveyed the kids in the room and spotted Blake, leaning against the doorframe. Distracting enough she nearly forgot her point. "But when we respect someone else—what they need, where they want to go, what their goals are—we can feel good that we gave them a helping hand.

"It's easy to recognize how someone else influenced us or made our life better. It's easy to be selfish and expect everyone else to help us. But it takes character to look for how you can help others get what *they* want."

She waved at Drew. "A car means Drew can go chase what he wants elsewhere." One of the kids made a comment under their breath about what Drew was chasing, but she ignored it. "A car means freedom from what's holding him back. Which is what we all want."

She walked to the side of the room and got a chair, then she set it facing Austin and sat across the table from him. Because fair was fair, she said, "Drew needs a car. What do you need?"

"For this to be over." The teen shot her a disgruntled look and shifted in his chair, frustrated with all this. Over it.

"What can we do to help you?" He'd signed a contract, like they all did when they joined the center, to see a tribunal through to its conclusion. Giving the kids ownership of this place and creating a sort of membership let them feel like they belonged. And when they belonged to something, it could feel like family.

Everyone wanted to be accepted. To know they were a part of something.

These kids maybe more than most.

A shadow of something flashed dark in Austin's eyes.

Violet kept her voice soft, in case he wanted to talk without anyone else hearing. "What is it?"

He looked aside. Shrugged.

"Tell me what's going on?"

This was no longer about the deal Austin and Drew had made. Or the fact Drew had brought a gun into the center. The consequences of that wouldn't be passed over. She couldn't allow lethal weapons in here.

"Haven't seen my brother. Can't find him." He sniffed.

"When did you see him last?"

Austin said, "Couple of days."

Violet had a colleague whose husband was a homicide detective. She usually stayed out of the circle of first responders in Benson, despite her connection through work. The last thing she wanted was for anyone to put together the pieces of who she was. She liked her day job to be separate from this. Still, for the sake of giving Austin peace of mind, maybe she could at least call around and see if anyone had seen his brother.

"Can you give me his info? First and last name, date of birth, and his phone number?"

Austin's expression twisted. "You gonna call the cops?"

"I have a friend connected to Vanguard and the police department. Why not use those resources and let me help you find him?" She shrugged. "Unless you think he maybe just split town for a couple of days."

Austin said, "Wouldn't be the first time."

"I can at least put some feelers out. See if something might've happened to him." If a loved one of hers disappeared—or went missing—she would move mountains to get them back. But apart from colleagues at work and a tenuous relationship with her father and his wife, who exactly did she have in her life to get that worried about?

She should feel grief over that, but it was for the best.

Austin said, "I'll give you his number. But I don't want cops lookin' for Marco."

"You got it." She pushed her chair back. "I'm happy to help if I can."

"So that's it?" One of the girls uncrossed her legs and leaned forward on her chair in the front row. "They're just going to leave the deal alone, forget it?"

Drew nodded. Austin did the same.

"Looks that way." Violet glanced around.

The girl stood. "It's a good idea. If they can agree on terms." She looked at the other girls she'd been sitting with and said, "Let's go," then walked over to Violet. "We're gonna catch a movie at the cheap seats."

"Fun," Violet said. "Be safe."

The girls all shook their keys—most of which had cans of palm-sized pepper spray. A few times, Violet had thought about calling the company across town that did private security. Getting Vanguard to come in and teach a self-defense class for all the kids, not just the girls, could be an invaluable experience.

No one wanted to be vulnerable. They were plenty smart, but life didn't always go the way anyone planned.

Like meeting a guy on a random weekday at her volunteer gig and being completely blown away by him. *Except that he's gone now.*

Drew pushed his chair back.

Austin said, "I'll text you my brother's info, but you're gonna hit Drew for that gun. Right?"

"I have that covered also." She nodded.

Drew sat on the table. The rest of the kids filed out, including Austin.

"If I hire someone to teach the girls self-defense, you think the guys will be interested?"

Drew blinked. Not what he had been expecting her to start with.

"We all need to know how to protect ourselves," she said.

"Could put it to committee. See if we can get it in the budget," Drew said.

"Maybe I can ask, and someone will do it for free." She shrugged. "Would that get you to leave illegal weapons alone? You know the risk of getting caught with a gun on you. Is it worth it?" He needed to feel strong and in control. That was why he'd brought a gun to confront Austin. So there was no way he'd leave without his money.

Drew said nothing.

"I get that you make your own choices, but this place exists to help you." If the kids didn't believe in it, then she'd failed here. Kind of like she'd failed everywhere else in her life.

And wasn't that the real issue?

Drew had brought a gun rather than ask for a tribunal. Which meant he didn't trust the center. Maybe he was only here while he marked time and kept saving so he could buy a car and get away from his life. Maybe he was the reason why some money from the safe had gone missing a couple of months ago—the thief never revealed.

She'd stopped leaving money inside, so temptation had nothing to satisfy it.

Drew slid off the table to stand. "I don't need help."

"Don't bring a gun here. You're walking a fine line, and you won't get another shot at sticking around." Violet needed him to understand the stakes here. "Success or failure is entirely up to you. Don't make the wrong choice."

SIX

Blake wiped his hand on a napkin so he could push the earbud in a little more. If it fell out, it would end up between the front seats of his department-issued unmarked vehicle. The Toyota liked to eat stray items, and he'd lost enough change, notes he'd written, and even a debit card.

The gun Lettie had taken from Drew remained in the brown paper bag on the front passenger's seat. As soon as he finished his lunch, he would turn it in to be processed.

She didn't need to know he'd taken it, but he'd tell her if she asked.

"Part of me wants to never go back there again." He made a face, then took another bite of the sub sandwich he'd bought on the way back to the office. Not much of a dinner, but it would do for now.

Liam's face filled the screen. Their video call was an appointment they both kept. Sure, Blake could talk to Jasper, but there was something...steady about Liam these days. Probably because he'd found Roxie—and religion.

His friend glanced at something off-screen, then back at Blake. "You really want to avoid her that much?"

Blake hadn't been surprised when Liam got right to the point. "The connection to the case is loose. I'm going to look up their finances when I get to my desk, but there's no indication she's involved. The two guys I met playing ball need to take their business elsewhere."

They were likely there to recruit vulnerable kids to work for them in exchange for cash. That wasn't their base of operations.

"Need your help," Liam said to someone else, then he lifted his chin. "What did you say it was called?"

Blake frowned. "Benson Fresh Start Center for Teens."

"Got it." The voice belonged to a woman, and it wasn't Roxie. "Full financials?"

Liam said, "Yes, ma'am."

"You have people now?"

Liam snorted. "Talia is NSA and is on the taskforce. Her husband is Secret Service, local office—financial crimes, mostly." He grinned. "It's her world, we're all just living in it."

"Ain't that right," this Talia person called from off-screen. "But for the record, it won't take me the rest of your explanation of how amazing I am to find what you need. I already have the full tax filing from the Benson Fresh Start Center for Teens."

When she came into view, Blake had to blink. "Hey."

"Hey yourself there, baby." Her smile was polite and professional but warm. "Whatever you need, Talia is here. But I'll have to dig below the surface if you wanna find out what this place is about. Their finances are public record, but that doesn't always tell the whole story of how it's run. If I get under the surface, I should be able to tell you if the center is clean or dirty."

He nodded. "'preciate it."

"Anything for a friend of Liam's." She winked, then a phone in the background chimed. "I'm gonna kill that kid. Startin' fights at daycare like he's a thug." She rolled her chair out of sight. "Mama gon' sit you down and talk to you, boy."

Liam grinned.

"Good team?"

"The best."

Blake smiled, but that hurt. They'd worked SWAT together for years, and he'd felt like they were a family. The one he'd never had at home, where he took the responsibility and the brunt of the work. The girls' mom had wanted him around as long as he was useful to her.

After she died, he took the role of both parents and raised the younger ones. Now, Hope lived with an aunt and was almost done with high school. The kid was so responsible she already had a full ride worked out for college.

His teammates on SWAT hadn't expected him to do everything for them. They'd shared the load equally, and Blake had loved not being the ranking cop. Liam had been his sergeant, best he'd ever had. Gage was a great lieutenant. Blake, Jasper, and their teammate, Dakota, who had quit to spend time in rehab and get himself straight, had worked great together.

Now, it was like they'd been hit by a meteor. Struck with the decision to turn SWAT from a full-time team into a part-time detail that he was still part of—but which looked nothing like it had. Flung in all different directions.

Even if he put on that SWAT uniform and got to work, it wouldn't be the same.

He'd had it good for a while, but, go figure, it hadn't lasted. Good never did. Life had taught him that. It was why he didn't talk to any of his friends about Christianity when they brought it up. Why get sucked in with all the hope and promises if it was only a matter of time before it all came crashing down?

Liam said, "I'll pass over what Talia found. Looks like there's a foundation that gives money to the center regularly. Keeps it going."

"Could be money laundering." Though, he doubted it. "And thanks. Tell her I said thanks also."

"You're welcome!" Her call came from off-screen.

Liam grinned. "Anytime, Blake. I'm serious."

Blake nodded.

"And you should just go give that girl your number. Got it?" Liam's amusement dropped from his expression, replaced by an earnestness Blake didn't see often. "Life is too short to hang around and not go after something you want. I learned that the hard way, and now I'm making up for lost time."

Liam and Roxie had admitted how they felt just a few months ago. Since then, they'd taken new jobs, and their relationship seemed to have moved along at light speed.

Blake wasn't in such a hurry to complicate his life, even if he could do it without the fallout of admitting where he'd come from.

"I'll have to tell her I'm a cop," Blake said. "Not sure she holds police in high esteem."

"So show her who you are. It'll change her mind." Liam shrugged, like doing that was no big deal.

Blake swallowed against the lump in his throat. "Gotta go." Or he'd end up getting all emotional about how much he appreciated Liam. He hung up the video call and tapped into the thread with his sisters. Hope was doing her statistics homework and was stuck on a problem. He figured it out and told her where she was going wrong.

Before he hit send, his phone started to ring.

He finished the text and answered the call while climbing out of the car and going for the back door of the department. "Blake Reed."

He needed to run the foundation that regularly donated money to keep the center doors open. Hopefully not money laundering, but he, of all people, knew that nothing was as it seemed.

"Son." The voice sounded deep and rich with a touch of gravel.

That same ache pounded in his chest, causing Blake to need to take a deep breath. He swiped his key card for the entry door. "Hey, Pops." He pushed in the door. "You got my message?"

"Don't need one to have a reason to call my boy." In the background of the call, Blake could hear more than one person talking and a loud buzzer.

The inside of the state penitentiary never quieted. How did his dad even stand it? Blake would never have survived.

"You can tell Jas to pass the guy's information to the warden. I'll make the approach. See if he'll talk to the cops."

In prison, that would brand his father as a police sympathizer. "It'll put a target on you."

"I'll feel him out slow, son. Don't worry. My life is in His hands. Always has been."

The warmth in his father's voice made Blake want to find a quiet corner of the PD so he could shut his eyes and just listen. But soaking it up wasn't something he could afford to do.

Blake gripped the phone. He stopped in the entryway to Intelligence because no one else was around. "I don't want you to put yourself at risk of getting hurt."

The prison was far more dangerous than being out on the

streets as a cop. His dad faced down the danger every day and told Blake often that God was the one in control.

"What I'm here for."

Blake asked, "Everything else okay?" because he had to get back to work.

"You know," his dad reassured him, meaning all was good. Same old. "Bible study is going great. I know I'm exactly where God wants me to be."

Too bad Blake couldn't say the same about his own life.

SEVEN

Violet lifted her hand and knocked on the door. Freya shifted up beside her to lean on the wall by the apartment door. Watching her back. "You could've stayed in the ambulance. I wouldn't have minded."

Freya rolled her shoulders. "Too much sitting already this shift. And after a day doing homework for my anatomy class, I needed the stretch."

Her partner this shift was working on getting her nursing degree. They'd known each other nearly seven years, worked together on and off, and Freya was the one who'd led Violet to her faith in God. She wasn't going to argue with a woman who seemed relentless in her desire to be friends even if they didn't get to see each other much.

The door opened. A midtwenties woman with perfectly curled hair and tired eyes said, "Yeah?" immediately followed by, "I didn't call you."

"We know." They were on their lunch break, but it was after ten at night. "Sorry to knock so late. I volunteer at the shelter downtown with Marco's brother, Austin. He's pretty worried. Have you seen Marco?"

As far as Austin had told her, he lived here sometimes when he cared enough to remember his girlfriend had given birth to two of his children. Or it was just that he was out of alternate places to crash.

"Marco?" The girlfriend rolled her eyes. "I haven't seen that waste of space since I threw his stuff in the stairwell and told him not to come back. He's actually doing it this time, so don't ruin that for me."

"Any idea where I can—"

The girlfriend cut her off. "Haven't seen him. Don't wanna see him."

She shut the door in their faces.

Violet blinked.

"Right, then." Freya pushed off the wall. "Smoothies or milkshakes?"

Violet headed to the stairwell so they could go down to the first floor. "This time of night?"

"Ooh, milkshakes and fries." Freya made an appreciative sound. "That sounds good."

"Because you're married, so you don't have to worry about being four thousand pounds and having a backside the size of a bus."

Freya snorted. "Sure. Just about the time the ink dries on your marriage license, you can start to let yourself go. Have you seen my husband? I don't wanna be the middle-aged spreading woman with scraggly hair and wrinkles standing next to that. I've got to be intimidating and fabulous so no one tries to steal him."

Violet pulled open the front door. "You really worry?"

"About him? No." Freya strode out into the courtyard. "No way. Lucas would never. But that doesn't mean I don't worry about all those ladies who'd snap him up in a heartbeat."

Violet got in the passenger's side of the ambulance cab and climbed into the seat, shifting her radio from her hip to lay on her lap. She usually kept the strap across her body, but right now she needed to unzip her fleece-lined jacket. Freya liked to crank the heat while they drove around—a throwback to growing up in Malaysia, probably. Washington winters could be frigid, but mostly, it was only wet, not snowing. That happened up in the mountains.

"Food, and we keep looking until a call comes in?"

"Sure." Violet checked her cell phone and texted Austin so he'd know she was working the problem. She told him that Marco's girlfriend hadn't seen him anytime recently.

Freya hit the button for the radio preset that played a national Christian radio station. Worship music poured through the speakers, bringing with it a kind of familiar peace Violet needed right now. Plus, it had been a long day, so the music would keep them both engaged while singing along.

"What else is going on with you?"

Did Violet want to talk about the mysterious hot guy she'd met that morning? Nope. "Tribunal. It worked out, and now we're helping Austin."

"Because fair's fair?"

Violet nodded, resisting the urge to grab the handle at the top of the door. Freya probably wouldn't crash the ambulance and kill them both, but it would be close.

"Hate to break it to you, but that's not teaching them how the real world works."

Violet said, "They know how the world works. I want to give them a reprieve from it, not more lessons that there's nothing they can do when they get the shaft. Or that when they're wronged, the only way to respond is with street justice."

"Well, when you put it like that..."

Violet grinned. "Do justly. Love mercy."

"And walk humbly," Freya said. "We should get that as tattoos."

Violet laughed. "Matching tattoos?"

"Okay, maybe not. But if I'm going to get a verse inked on me permanently, I can't think of many that are better."

"I'd have to think about it," Violet said. "I still don't have a life verse."

Freya let go of the steering wheel to wave a hand. "I've had so many I've lost count. Right now, it's 'My head is drenched with dew, my hair with the dampness of the night.' But that's just because it rained yesterday."

Violet laughed.

"What are you reading right now?"

"I'm still doing the same plan," Violet said. "The Old Testament once and the New Testament twice in one year." She'd started it in the summer, so even though it was January, she was halfway through. She tapped on the app for her internet browser and pulled up the verse she'd looked up from a phrase she remembered. "I really like in Hebrews chapter ten where it says to draw near 'with a sincere heart and with the full assurance that faith brings.' You know, sincerity of heart and confidence in the hope we have?"

It was keeping her going right now when she didn't have much else in her life that was going well. She almost felt like she was in a holding pattern—or about to level up somehow. Things were plodding along fine, and she could be content most of the time.

Work was good. The shelter was where she was making a difference. Both saved lives in different ways.

Maybe a part of her wondered if there was more.

But that just made her feel ungrateful.

Freya hit the turn signal for the drive-through place that

was open late, the one that specialized in shakes and fries. As she pulled in, a thunderous blast erupted in the distance followed by an orange fireball.

Violet gripped the dash.

Freya pulled into a space instead of the drive-through. Both of them would wait and see if whatever had just happened resulted in them being called out. They weren't far away, but if they went before they were given the address, they would only get in the way of whoever was responding.

"I was going to say something about being sure of your faith," Freya said. "Now I can't remember."

Freya had been a firm believer when they met on shift just like this, and Violet had finally opened up about how she got here. Since then, Freya had gone through a crisis of faith. They'd been partnered with other people, and now they only worked together on the rare occasion that the department needed Freya to fill a spot on a shift, which wasn't often.

Freya had met Lucas and renewed her faith. They were married. She was embarking on a new journey in more ways than one.

Meanwhile, nothing much had changed for Violet.

Maybe it never would.

The dash radio cut through an upbeat chorus. "Bus fourteen, explosion. Adolescent victim." The dispatcher relayed the address.

Violet hit the transmission button. "Bus fourteen responding."

They pulled up two minutes later behind a fire truck, which was surrounded by firefighters battling a fire. The place was a complex of storage units, and the middle row had an open roof through which flames licked up into the sky.

"A kid was in there?" Freya put the ambulance in park.

"I hope not." It looked like someone had reached down

and torn open one of the units. If the hand had a fifteen-foot palm span. When they'd made their way to the command chief, pushing the stretcher between them with their gear bags on top, she asked, "Where do you want us?"

"Kid is over there." The fire captain shook his head. "Messing around. They shoulder checked the wrong unit, roughhousing. It blew from the inside."

"Like a bomb?" Violet asked.

He nodded. "It must've been wired up to prevent entry. The two of them are lucky to be in one piece."

They pushed the gurney toward two firefighters and two preteen boys, who were lying on the ground. Crying. Blood.

Freya said, "Remember when we didn't get called out to explosions and bombings?"

Violet nodded. They'd dealt with a nightclub bombing together a while back, maybe a couple of years ago. Then a limo exploded over the summer—but Violet hadn't been on shift during that.

Times had certainly changed in Benson.

EIGHT

Blake gripped the remote for his drone, the sweat on his brow chilling in the morning frost. It had dipped below freezing to make each breath puff out in front of his face. Barely five in the morning and they'd been in their SWAT uniforms for more than an hour—long enough to make the plan and get over here with their warrant.

"Anything?" Lieutenant Gage Deluca patted his shoulder.

Blake shifted in his SWAT boots, and all the gear on his vest creaked. "Nothing in the back rooms. Moving to the hall now so I can search the front living areas."

"He's probably hiding because he knows we're out here." Officer Gutierrez thought he was hilarious, apparently.

Omara didn't seem so amused. Or Jasper. Neither said anything over the radio from their spots covering the rear of the house.

Blake stared at the screen of the laptop, navigating the drone through the house. It saw infrared, so they knew whether someone was inside or not before they even breached. And given the fact a storage unit had exploded last night because two kids slammed against the door, no one was taking chances here.

"Get me a look at the front door."

"Copy that." Blake navigated the drone in that direction and turned it. "Looks wired up."

"So, we go in the window you used? Or the back door?"

Jasper was the one who'd cut away a section of glass to send the drone inside. The back door hadn't been wired up.

"He was counting on us coming in the front." Blake studied the wiring. "You think we need the bomb squad?" Benson had a group that consisted of two officers and two firefighters who had the training it took to safely deal with an explosive device. Whoever was on shift—or could get over to the site fastest with their bomb suit—got the task of disarming any device that was found.

"No time." The lieutenant tipped his head. "I've taken the same training, and I coordinate the team now."

Blake gritted his teeth. Gage, his lieutenant, had married Clare, who ran Vanguard Private Security and Investigations, a few months ago. They were pregnant with their first child already. Not that the lives of anyone who didn't have kids was less valuable, but Blake didn't like the idea of his friend and supervisor taking that risk.

"Come on." Gage said over the radio, "We're breaching, side windows and rear door. No one touches the front. It's rigged. Watch for trip wires or any other surprises." The lieutenant strode off toward the back of the house.

Blake continued to fly the drone around the house. "I'm not seeing any other doors wired up. Or signs anyone is inside." His voice carried over the open comms, and he kept his focus on the screen. The four cops here would breach the house, and Blake was more like overwatch in this situation—

plus keeping an eye on the street in case anyone showed up after the others had gone inside.

This was way more of what he wanted to do and where he felt like he belonged as opposed to Intelligence. Probably, he should've gone into the military. But after their mom died, the girls had been adrift. If he'd been out of the country and potentially out of contact for long periods, none of them would've been okay. Especially not him.

That was probably the most significant issue he had with Destiny and her need to follow her heart to what she called a "mission trip" in Africa. He didn't even know what that meant.

Blake navigated the drone to a corner he hadn't checked yet. Sometimes, he'd clear a whole house before anyone went in.

Gage gave the order to breach, and the lieutenant led the other three officers inside.

Blake's mind still wouldn't let go of the fact Sergeant Deerdan would likely order him to get close to Hound and Pat for the sake of the case. To get them to trust him so he could figure out the scope of their operation and how it connected to the three dead dealers they had on their hands.

More undercover work.

He'd rather be wearing a helmet and vest, breaching a house.

"Contact!" Jasper's callout cut off, descending into a series of thuds and thumps.

Blake landed the drone in a corner and set the remote down. He raced around the house and through the open back door, gun ready. Someone had attacked Jasper. Where had the suspect come from?

He found his friend in the hall and spotted blood on the outside of Jasper's arm. In front of him, Officer Jesse had the suspect subdued with Lieutenant Deluca covering him. All of them had dark expressions.

"Where did he come from?"

Gutierrez strode in from another room. "Study is clear. The whole house is clear. Or we *thought* it was." He shot Blake a look.

Blake held his gun against his chest. "The drone picked up no heat signatures in the house."

Jasper pushed off the wall and moved past Blake, who followed him to the hall closet.

"He was in there?" If that was the case, the drone should've picked him up unless the walls were somehow lined in order to disguise him.

Jasper waved his good arm. "He came out of here."

Blake stepped inside and pushed back the row of coats on hangars. Behind them, where the wall should be, was an open hatch. He ducked in and spotted it. "He hid in a freezer."

The lid was open. Blake flipped on the flashlight on the end of his rifle under the barrel and swept it around the tiny storage area behind the cupboard.

"How'd he get a freezer in there?" Jasper's voice was tight.

Blake surveyed the blood. "We need to get you to the hospital."

Lieutenant Deluca appeared behind Jasper. "Ambulance is on its way. You can see your doc later. And the bomb on the front door is disabled, by the way. If anyone is curious."

Blake fought the pull of a grin. "Thanks, LT."

"We're taking the suspect outside." Deluca stepped over to Jesse. "Gutierrez, get an idea of where we want the crime scene folks to start processing."

Officer Gutierrez nodded. "Copy that, LT."

Jasper took a step, stumbled, and started to keel over.

Blake caught him. "I've got you."

"Thanks, brother." His tight voice sounded thin now.

Blake held Jasper's weight and walked him to the front door, even though it made him nervous to pass the explosive device. A few neighbors had gathered on the sidewalk to see what the early morning commotion was. Gage shooed them back and took command of the scene as lieutenant.

An ambulance pulled up, and he walked his friend to it. If the man who'd been hiding was the subject of the warrant, this would be a win, even with Jasper's injury. Who else would've been hiding aside from the man who'd wired up the front door and a storage unit?

Blake didn't know of any open cases about bombings and wasn't sure if the case of the limousine that'd exploded over the summer had been closed. Was it the same case? He wouldn't be asking, because no one he worked with needed to know he had a kind of fascination with explosive devices.

Not with his history.

He tried to keep both on the down low. No one needed to even wonder if the son of Jamal Reed wanted to learn how bombs worked. So he'd never volunteered to take that course or become an expert, even if the goal was to disarm, not destroy.

The two female EMTs strode to the back of the ambulance.

One was Freya, whose husband was a homicide detective. The other...

Blake nearly stumbled. "Lettie?"

She blinked, starting as she scanned his face. "Blake."

"I'm bleeding," Jasper said. "It's nice to meet you."

Freya chuckled. "Come on, Hollingsworth. We'll get you wrapped up so you can get back to being a hero." She took the weight of his friend, and Jasper sat on the back of the ambulance. "Violet, make sure he doesn't fall over while I get the bag."

Lettie moved to Jasper.

Blake did the same. "Violet?" Was that like a stage name?

She winced, her smooth dark features flashing with an unreadable expression. Not much about it seemed guilty. But it was clear she didn't like this.

That made two of them.

"Lettie is kind of a nickname. Violet is my...legal name. And you didn't tell me you're a cop."

"And you didn't tell me you're an EMT."

"She's a paramedic, actually." Freya knelt beside Jasper and lifted his elbow. He looked about ready to pass out. "On account of all the medical training she's had."

Violet winced. "We don't need to talk about that."

Blake folded his arms across his chest. "Disagree."

"I'm working. And so are you." Violet turned to Jasper. "Now isn't the time for this."

"Fine," Blake said. "When do you get off shift?"

NINE

"That's the one." The lousy attempt at a whisper came from behind the nurses' station in the Emergency Department.

Violet strode past with the jump bag of supplies she'd restocked.

"Jasper Hollingsworth." The nurse's tone was full on Victorian-era vapors. "His father is a state senator."

Blake stepped out of the middle bay ahead of her and stared. No motion for her to come to him or any indication he wanted to speak to her. All he did was watch her approach. As if he had the right to be madder than she was. He'd lied to her. Misrepresented who he was.

Which was totally different from the fact that not many of the people who frequented the center knew of her day job.

Now that she'd figured out who he was, the stories his sisters had told her about the brother who raised them made her stop in front of him. Set the bag by the wall.

Give him at least a minute to say what he wanted to say.

Long enough for Freya to return from the vending machines, and then she'd be out of here, back to her life.

"Violet." His tone was dark. "That's what you go by as an EMT, while at the center you lie and tell everyone your name is Lettie? Have I got that right?"

She bit the inside of her lip. Out of respect for his sisters, she would hear him out. She wouldn't fly off the handle.

Rage was a symptom, not her problem.

"I don't lie to anyone about who I am." She had no idea where he stood on faith, but most people would agree that lying was bad. "Maybe we should just let this go. Neither of us was completely honest about who we are." She shrugged, but her heart wasn't in it. "It's not like there's a 'thing.'"

"Is that really what you want?"

Violet stepped back and looked into the bay. "What I want isn't usually a factor."

She felt a light touch on her shoulder and glanced at him, finding every inch the big brother the girls loved.

Before he could speak, she said, "I see what the girls mean."

All of them talked about their big brother, Blake, and how he did everything to keep them safe. How he'd helped with their homework, reminded them to do laundry before they had no clean clothes, and picked them up when they needed a ride home.

This man was all cop, SWAT and lethal in a second when the occasion called for it, but beneath that was a good man who cared.

One she wanted to know.

Along with getting answers to all her other questions.

"So, you live a double life." He looked as intrigued by her as she was by him.

"And you work undercover." Something that maybe should've been obvious clicked in her mind. "Who are you investigating?"

He'd been at the center for a reason. Was it her, someone else there, or the organization in general? She wasn't informed on the day-to-day financial operations. Violet preferred to be more people-focused.

After all, she had a lot to make up for. Not to earn anything but to keep giving. To be characterized as someone who did good, regardless of the guilt and shame she should feel.

She studied the reticence on his face. "Or can you not tell me because the case involves me?" Her stomach flipped over. Why would she be the subject of an investigation?

"The center connects to more than one case." He tipped his head to the side. "But we don't know how or if it's simply a coincidence."

His attention shifted behind her.

Violet turned and spotted his lieutenant coming this way.

He held out his hand as he approached. "Gage Deluca."

"Violet." She shook his hand, hoping neither noticed that she hadn't used her last name. "Nice to meet you, Lieutenant." The bars on his shoulders were a dead giveaway.

Blake asked, "Anything new?"

"Got the suspect booked in." Gage nodded. "Ran his prints since he had no ID and wasn't talking."

"Our bomb maker?" Blake asked.

So that was who they'd been going after this morning. Violet glanced at the clock. It was time to get Freya and take the ambulance back to the firehouse for the day shift medics.

Gage said, "Nope. Prints came back as Marco Phelps."

Violet flinched. The assailant in that house had been Austin's brother?

Both cops noticed—of course, they noticed. Much to her father's dismay, she couldn't school her features in the heat of the moment. Though, with her history, that was the least of her worries.

Lord, I hope You know what You're doing with me.

"So, what was he doing hiding in a closet, in a freezer?" Blake shook his head.

Violet frowned.

Blake noticed. "I'll tell you later."

Gage didn't miss that comment.

As far as she could see, they wouldn't have a "later."

Sure, she was intrigued enough to want to get to know him. But now that she knew who he was, the guy was way more intimidating than he already had been. He would never consider her someone worth having in his life for the long term.

"Local guy," Gage said. "Petty stuff, mostly, but in a way where he was primed to get into more serious stuff. He was either stealing from the guy or crashing there to learn from him."

"Like an apprentice?" Blake asked.

"Maybe," Gage said. "We'll find out when he starts talking. His lawyer should be in soon."

They both shifted, like they were going to go into the ER bay where the nurse was feeling around Jasper's cut. He looked like he wanted to be sick.

"Hold up." Violet lifted both hands. "Bombs? And Austin's brother? You guys are still looking for the guy who makes the devices, right?"

Thankfully, she hadn't gone inside the house. They were brave to have done so. She'd seen the destruction of the storage unit. It was a miracle no one had been killed. However, many people's lives were forever changed, even with only an injured child and his friend involved.

"Sure, we're looking for him." Gage took a half step away.

"But we need intel, or we're looking for a ghost. We need Marco to tell us who this guy is and how they know each other. Then we can get all the cops in Benson looking for him before the next bomb goes off and the worst happens."

Violet blinked. "You're sure one will?"

"In my experience, things get worse before they get better." Gage glanced at Blake, then at her. "I'm gonna go talk to Jas."

Violet needed to tell Austin—and maybe also the ex-girlfriend—that Marco had been arrested. She'd found his brother, but Austin might not like what had happened to him. The people she tried to help often weren't fans of the police. What would happen to their trust in her if she started spending a lot of time with cops? She hadn't even admitted to them she was a paramedic.

Freya strode up. "Hey." She turned to Violet. "Ready to go?"

She had more questions, but that had to be tempered with the question of when she would see Blake again. Or *if* she would.

Blake asked, "Do my sisters know you're an EMT?"

Freya slung an arm around Violet's shoulders. "I'm the EMT. She's a paramedic because of all her medical training—"

Violet poked her friend in the side.

"Make some space." The nurse squeezed around them.

"How is he?" Blake asked. "And when will he get stitched up? We've been here forever."

The nurse said, "The chief of surgery is coming down personally to do it." She glanced at Freya and Violet. "For some reason."

Did she know?

Violet nudged Freya's arm off her shoulder. "We should

go." She stepped back, caught her foot before the rubber sole on the waxed floor caused her to stumble, and turned. "Later, guys."

She didn't need to be here when her father came down from the lofty heights of his kingdom to grace the little people with his presence.

The nurse held their paperwork up over the counter. "All done. I've got you covered."

They were covering for her now? "Thanks." Violet choked on the word and had to clear her throat.

Freya strode out between the automatic doors first. Violet glanced back at Blake, who stood in that same spot, staring at her.

She tried not to care what he thought. Tried not to be intrigued enough to want to walk back there and do a fool thing like give him her phone number.

That was the last thing she needed to do. Her life was already complicated enough. Her cup was full.

Beyond him, the elevator doors slid open, and a tall man in a white coat stepped out.

Violet sidestepped out the door.

Out of sight.

TEN

Blake had the file in hand as he headed down the hall between Intelligence and the department behind it. Between the two were interview rooms everyone used. And the break room—but he'd already had too much coffee.

He'd need a power nap later, but for now, it was time to ask Marco Phelps a whole lot of questions in the hope of getting some answers.

Given that the two incidents were related to explosive devices—though only one had gone off—every commanding officer in the Benson PD had an eye on this case. His sergeant waited in the hall outside the interview room. Megan Deerdan didn't look at all like she'd been woken up before dawn with news of an arrest and a possible bomb threat, although she had less makeup on today than she did at other times.

She stepped back. "Got it, Detective?"

"Yes, Sergeant." He handed her the file and went in first. After not having much of a relationship with his mother, who drank when she wasn't working and didn't do much else, he appreciated the sergeant's no-nonsense demeanor.

She sat at the table. "Mr. Phelps, you were arrested in the course of us serving a warrant to ascertain the identity of the owner of a storage unit that was packed to the gills with explosive devices." She flipped open the paper file and scanned down the page. "The same kind that had been wired up behind the door of the house."

Marco leaned back in his chair, the expression on his face blank. He wanted them to believe he didn't care about any of this. Other than the fact it was an inconvenience. "Not my bombs."

"During the course of us serving this warrant," the sergeant said, "you resisted arrest and assaulted a police officer that resulted in stitches." She informed Marco of his situation and his legal right to an attorney.

Blake glanced between the sergeant and the guy across the table. Sergeant Deerdan was more than capable of matching Marco's stubbornness. Her two boys must have had a hard time getting away with anything under her watch.

Blake's mom had been emotionally and physically weak, her struggle ending when she suffered a heart attack right before he turned nineteen. He'd already known about the girls then. They were his mom's favorite thing to gripe about...

He'd been there to help, give them some money, and make their lives better. Then, after mom died, he'd adopted them until most were out of the house, and then the youngest two had gone to live with their aunt. They'd still been at his house all the time even after that.

He liked his makeshift family.

Marco Phelps sat back in his chair, the brother of that teen who'd stolen from the other teen—the subject of the tribunal.

Another family that was small and dysfunctional.

Which only made his thoughts drift back to Violet. What was her family situation like? There had to be a reason she worked at the center when she wasn't a paramedic. Now that he knew more about her, he realized everything she did was about helping people—saving lives.

And then there was the chief of surgery who'd come down personally to stitch up Jasper.

Marco leaned forward. "Not. My. Bombs." He sat back and shrugged. "Charge me for stabbing the pretty boy, and let's be done with this."

"Not yet," the sergeant said.

Blake listened to her explain that they could reduce the charges for what happened with Jasper in exchange for his cooperation about what was going on with the bombs. Dr. George Anderson, the chief of surgery who'd come down, had borne a striking resemblance to Violet. They had the same coloring, the same facial features. Even their mannerisms were similar.

The doctor with the silk shirt and the expensive shoes had reminded him distinctly of...his daughter? Was that who she was?

She'd run off after hearing the guy was on his way. Whatever it was couldn't be good. He wanted to listen to the story from her, not from a gossiping third party.

"Detective Reed?"

Blake blinked. Instead of admitting he'd zoned out—due to a mix of fatigue and Violet—he asked, "Why don't you tell me about the freezer?"

She probably hadn't brought that up yet since she'd started with the identity of the man who lived at the house.

Marco showed a slight flash of fear, there for a second and then gone. "So the guy had a freezer, so what?"

"How'd you know it was in the closet?" The guy was lucky to be alive, but Blake had enough near misses that he could say the same thing. "You've been in the house before, right?"

Marco sniffed. "My supplier sent me there once to give him some money."

A payment. That was interesting. "So, you met him then?" But that didn't get Marco all the way to the freezer this morning. Had he been staying there, or was he just there for some other reason in the early hours?

"Once."

"Was he at the house last night?"

"I didn't see him." Marco's foot tapped on the floor. "When I heard you guys outside and that drone was coming through the house, I ducked into the closet, found the freezer, and hid inside. Until I couldn't breathe."

"How'd you know to hide in there?" His sergeant probably wanted him to ask about the bomb maker, but Blake would get there. He had his own way to question suspects—most cops did. A style that worked for him, except when it didn't. People were people. Tactics were good. But Blake's was based on how he wasn't so far removed from the guys across the table.

He got to be a cop, and he was grateful to be on this side of the desk, but he wasn't going to use that position to lord it over guys that could've so easily been him.

Marco shifted in his seat. "When I was there, delivering that payment...I mighta heard someone. Screaming."

"He had someone in there?"

Beside him, Sergeant Deerdan stiffened.

Marco said, "I never saw. But I heard her screaming."

Hence, he'd known to hide in there when the police showed up. "Why were you at his house today?"

"Not to get arrested."

Blake said nothing. His sergeant kept quiet as well.

"My supplier bought it a couple of weeks ago."

One of their victims? Blake waited for Marco to continue.

"I'm probably next." The guy sniffed, then adjusted his seat on the chair. "But that don't mean I don't got bills to pay."

"Does he hire guys like you for jobs?"

Marco shrugged. "Worth asking."

"Did you see him?" Blake and the PD hadn't been able to come up with much as to the identity of the man who rented both that house and the storage unit. A man proficient in crafting explosive devices should be on their radar—so how had he gone unchecked for so long?

"Not last night."

"Again. You've met him before."

A bomb maker with a captive woman in his house.

Sergeant Deerdan tapped the table with two fingers. "We want to find him, Marco. Enough that we're willing to persuade the DA that our cop doesn't care about how you sliced him. You could walk away from this, but that means you give us this guy."

They gave that a few seconds to sink in. This was a tricky situation. How would Jasper's father—the state senator—feel about an attack on his son going unpunished?

Then Blake said, "I need his name. I need a description. I need to know where to find him, and everything else you know. All of it."

Marco stared at him.

"You don't want Austin to grow up just like you, but you're in jail. That's where he's headed, so maybe you guys can be cellmates," Blake said. "Or you can change the course of both your lives. Give us what we need and then get out of

Benson. Start a new life somewhere else. Get a second chance. And give your family one as well."

ELEVEN

"And you just ran away out the door?"

Violet bent into a squat and pulled the pan of enchilada casserole out. She set it on the stove and closed the oven door, fanning herself with the glove. "We had to get the ambulance back to the firehouse."

Granny lifted one penciled eyebrow—better than Violet could ever do—and stretched the gold eye shadow. She slid onto a stool at the bar and eyed Violet.

"Well, we did."

"Don't kid a kidder, child." Granny lifted the glass of spinach smoothie and sipped.

Violet had gone to breakfast right from her shift and chatted with her sponsor. They didn't check in so often these days, but it was still necessary to touch base. He was a cop, but she'd managed to keep from asking about Blake.

That only meant all the thoughts about him built up until they spilled out with Granny as she recounted her shift. Then she'd claimed she was more tired than usual and fallen into bed, only to lie there most of the day and stare at the ceiling.

Seeing a certain police detective in her mind.

She'd slept barely enough, made dinner, and taken a shower. Now she had thrown on yoga pants and an oversized Benson FD sweater. She had her hair tied up and covered with a thin towel that tucked in at the back of her neck while her hair dried. "What did you do today?"

"Brunch with my Bible study group. I got the veggie omelet because I went to the gym this afternoon, after I ran errands. Then the grocery store." She waved a hand at the pantry. "It was a little chilly, but not too bad. It'll snow next week, probably."

Doris Anderson had a more active social life, could bench press more than Violet, and was eighty-two, for crying out loud. Then again, Violet had come from a long line of over-achievers.

And she'd grown up to be their biggest disappointment.

Meanwhile, Granny kicked butt, took names, and tended to clean the whole house while Violet was at work. "You should let me help you."

"I like to be useful."

Violet put some dinner for each of them into two shallow bowls and carried it over to the breakfast bar. She slipped in beside Granny and leaned over to kiss her cheek. "You don't have to earn your keep. We're a team. Let me hold up my end of the bargain."

Granny patted her knee. "Then get me the sour cream, Let."

"Sure thing." Violet grinned and also grabbed the cheese from the fridge.

They held hands, and Violet prayed a blessing over their food. When she said, "Amen," Granny didn't. Violet opened her eyes and saw her grandmother's lips moving as she continued to pray by herself. She waited on her grand-mother, and when she was done, she asked, "Praying for wisdom on how to deal with your wayward granddaughter?"

Granny chuckled, the shimmery eye shadow giving her a glint in her eyes.

"Or..."

"Not your father."

She wouldn't lie, but if he were her son, Violet would pray for his wayward soul. She needed wisdom to deal with her dad, but if she continued to avoid him, she wouldn't have to ask for it. All she had to do was keep *not* running into him at the hospital.

There was no way that he'd come down last night to see her. Probably, he was trying to get on the good side of the PD. Or maybe descending from his lofty heights to remind people there were others who were better than them.

They started to eat, and after a few minutes, Violet said, "So, who were you praying for?"

"Detective Blake Reed. That was his name, wasn't it?"

Violet managed to keep the food in her mouth while she coughed. She swallowed against it and asked, "Blake?" She didn't sound too insane, so that was good. "Right. His sisters came into the center after school sometimes, when he had to work."

"So they told you about him?"

"We keep conversations about them. What they're going to do next, and who they're going to be." Violet shrugged one shoulder as if she felt at all casual. "Not their situations or what they've been through. We look forward, not back."

Granny said nothing.

Violet took another bite and chanced a look. *Don't kid a kidder.*

She didn't know why she bothered playing off anything. Maybe just to keep her grandmother from worrying. She might be healthier than most people half her age, but that didn't mean she could handle extreme stress. Not like what Violet had put her through years ago.

"Looking forward is good. Focusing on the future." Granny sipped her spinach drink. "Not living your life in a holding pattern like you don't want anything to happen."

Same old argument. "I love what I do and where I'm at."

"Taking care of an old lady?"

"What?!" Violet pretended she was aghast. "I thought you were taking care of me!"

Granny chuckled and smacked Violet's shoulder. "You're handy in a pinch. But that's not why I keep you around."

Violet leaned over and nudged the older woman's shoulder. "I know."

Too many times, her father had threatened to put Granny in a home or ship her off to Florida to some retirement community. As if anyone wanted to be in Florida in the summer. Talk about too hot to handle.

She'd seen the fear in her grandmother's eyes, but for a long time, she hadn't been able to do anything about it. When she hit rock bottom, Granny had suggested that Violet come live with her. Turns out, they both needed the company of a family member who had their back no matter what.

Granny finished her meal and leaned against Violet's shoulder. When Violet set her fork down, her grandmother asked, "Is he cute?"

Violet gasped.

"He is. I knew it." Granny nodded in that way all grannies did because they knew everything.

Violet pushed her bowl away and touched her forehead to the counter. "I ran away from Dad. Blake probably thinks I'm insane. *And* he's investigating the center."

"The Lord works in mysterious ways."

Violet lifted her head. "That's not even in the Bible, and you know it!" At least not phrased like that.

"Got your attention, though." Granny sipped her drink.

Violet just groaned.

"And He knows what He is doing." She patted Violet's knee again. "So you don't need to worry. Or try to force a result on your own. We all know how that turns out."

Hopefully, she was referencing a Bible story, but she likely wasn't when there was so much source material in Violet's past. She'd spent years trying to figure out what her life was, stripped of everything that had been piled on her shoulders.

She'd thrown it all off in one day.

Then she'd thrown herself off a bridge.

She'd given herself a concussion and a broken ankle and found a fresh start because God loved to show up at rock bottom and offer a second chance.

She glanced over. "Love you, Granny."

"Love you, too, girl."

Violet grabbed the bowls and stood.

"But you should still tell me what this guy is like."

Violet rinsed the dishes as if she didn't hear, since they'd already been over this—and Violet hadn't given her anything. Granny enjoyed being relentless.

When she glanced over her shoulder, Granny was on her cell phone, swiping the screen. That was a relief. Maybe it was indicative of a bit of senility that she'd jumped to an alternate distraction and forgotten her question, but—

"Ooh, he *is* cute."

Violet sprayed water on the front of her T-shirt. She hammered the faucet off and spun around, rushing over to look.

Her grandmother had pulled up the department's social

media page and searched his name to find a photo of the SWAT team from a couple of years ago.

"You can't even see his face that well." But she wanted to stare a little longer. Maybe zoom in.

Great. She was a creeper now.

The doorbell in the corner of the wall chimed with an alert for the front door. Probably a package, but Violet hadn't ordered anything in the last couple of days.

Granny pulled down the notification and tapped it. "I'll get a closer look." She held up her phone to show the camera. And Blake Reed was standing on their doorstep. "He's here." She slipped off the stool and nudged Violet to the hall. "I'll charm him. You change. And fix your hair!"

A nightmare. She was living in a nightmare.

Violet was half tempted to text her sponsor, but that could get sticky since he and Blake worked in the same precinct. It wasn't like this situation was driving her to make a choice that didn't fit with who she was now, even if the life of an addict was something she would never get past.

Never mind that she couldn't remember the last date she'd been on.

At least she didn't have to worry about faking it to impress him.

He'd met her father at the hospital. He had to have spoken with him. That meant one thing...

No way was he interested in her now.

If he ever had been.

TWELVE

"Yes, ma'am." Blake held in a grin. The trim old woman with the glint in her eye had that same Anderson resemblance to Violet that the chief of surgery had.

Where the doctor and his daughter seemed like oil and water, these two were more like peas in a pod. Gorgeous eyes, a spark of life in their expressions.

"Here you go." Doris Anderson handed him a mug of tea.

He spotted the living room, and what he saw there raised his eyebrows. That explained the light coming from there and bleeding into the kitchen.

Blake heard the swish of feet on the wood floor and turned to see Violet emerging from down the hall in jeans and a pink T-shirt that hugged her sides, her hair down around her shoulders. "Hey." He had to clear his throat.

"Hey yourself."

"There's tea for you, Let." Doris squeezed his elbow as she passed between them. "I'm headed to watch TV in my room. It's been a long day, and I'm tired."

Violet eyed her grandmother. Not concern. Her expression was more like suspicion.

Blake grinned and took a sip of the piping hot drink, burning his tongue. He must've made a noise because she said, "You don't have to drink that."

Violet reached for his mug.

Blake stepped back and swung it out of reach, thankfully not spilling it. "Don't take my tea. It's good."

"Just a thousand degrees?" When he nodded, she went to the fridge and dispensed two ice cubes into her hand, which she dropped into his mug.

"Thanks." He had to ask. "Um...do you still have your Christmas tree up?"

She beamed. "Of course! I love Christmas. Granny goes crazy baking and making presents for all her friends. After the first year, we decided to just keep it up all the time. All year round. We take the ornaments off in spring and then decorate it for each season. You should see some of my summer ones."

Blake stared at her.

"Let's go outside." She stepped back. "Then you can forget you saw it. You can pretend I'm normal."

"Why be normal? Where's the fun in that?"

She laughed. "The girls say that, right?"

He nodded.

"Come on. Seriously, you should see the porch."

Blake frowned at the temperature outside and the fact that both women assumed he'd come here to talk rather than anything more serious. But he was dressed in jeans, a sweater over a T-shirt, and a jacket. She would freeze outside with no warm layers on and in her bare feet.

Violet held the door open for him.

Blake eased past her, close enough to smell what she'd put

in her hair. It made him want to linger, but she said, "Hit that switch to your left. Both of them."

He found a panel of three buttons and pressed the first two. Fairy lights illuminated a porch with comfy looking chairs. A gas fire in the center flared to life. Warmth filled the area, beating back the chill coming through the glass windows around them. "A sunroom?"

Violet returned inside and got a blanket from a cupboard by the door. "Granny's idea. Another place to sit and 'be' as she says."

The couch creaked under him as he settled into it. Violet curled up next to him in the opposite corner. "Did you eat?"

He nodded. "How long have you lived with her?"

Violet blew out a breath, holding her mug with both hands but not drinking it. "Eight years, almost. She's a great roommate. Spunky, like Grace, and with a lot of heart, like Destiny." She grinned. "Have you heard from her?"

"Just a couple of emails to say she got there, and everything is okay. I figure she's busy. And the group she's with has a social media page, so I see their updates on that."

He didn't want to talk about Destiny or the fact she'd suddenly decided this fall to go to Africa on a mission trip for three months. She'd been there a few weeks now, and his heart still hadn't settled.

"She's a good kid. They all are."

Blake drank the tea.

"You don't have to pretend you like it."

"I'm not pretending!" He was drinking it, wasn't he? "It's good. It's just...orangey."

"Is that even a word?"

"It is now." He grinned and took another sip, then ended up coughing.

Violet laughed, a pleasant sound even if the edge was a

little uncertain. Because of him, or for another reason? Maybe she just didn't laugh a lot.

He apparently stared too long because she said, "What?"

He lifted one boot and put it on the brick edge of the gas fireplace. "So, you're a paramedic, you volunteer with teens at the center, and you live with your grandmother."

"And you're a police detective who raised four teenagers after their mom died, and everyone I've met that knows you respects the heck out of you."

He blinked. "They do?"

She nodded.

They knew a lot of the same people. Probably, they should've met before.

Had he missed something along the way, or had the girls made a point *not* to introduce them? He tried to figure out what he'd say on a text to the girls to indicate he'd met her and keep it light. But he'd have to do that later.

"You're investigating something, and it connects to the center?"

"I can't give out a lot of details about an ongoing case, but it relates to more than one murder investigation. Someone is killing dealers. One gunshot, one stab wound."

"Like someone is killing them twice?"

"More like sending a clear message to anyone who thinks to cross them." He couldn't say much more than that. "Which is putting everyone on edge—especially the department. No one wants more death. No matter who it is that's killed."

She said, "Some cops wouldn't care that dealers are dying. They'd just be glad they're dead and not worry about finding the culprit. Maybe they'd be hoping it's some kind of vigilante."

That was true enough. "I figure it's more like a power grab. Some new, and dangerous, player in town."

"Is this where you warn me to be careful?"

Blake's brows lifted. "Do I need to?"

She shook her head, a smile stretching her lips wide. "No. I'm careful, because Granny would tear me a new one if I wasn't."

Blake grinned. "I'm pretty sure she could take both of us."

"That's the truth." She frowned for a second. "I think I treated one of those dealers a few weeks ago."

"One of my vics?"

She nodded. "I took a guy to the ER in the ambulance. Shot and stabbed, once each. He looked like he might've been a dealer, though that's an assumption. Who knows?"

All three of the victims they were investigating had been discovered on the street. Who was this guy? "Can you pull up the paperwork and get me the information for that patient? Send me a copy. I need to look into it."

"Sure. I'll do it when I'm on shift tomorrow."

"Any idea if the guy made it?"

She shook her head. "He was headed for surgery, but it's not my job to get invested in their survival. I'm not supposed to do anything but try and keep them alive long enough to get treatment. I save the rest for the kids at the center."

"As someone who benefited from what you do at the center, I appreciate it. You do amazing work there. The girls speak highly of you."

"But they never introduced us."

Blake said, "I've been wondering the same thing. Guess we'll have to ask why."

They exchanged numbers, which turned out to be not as awkward as he'd thought. Why did he feel like a teenager with his first crush?

Probably because Violet was the first woman who'd interested him in a long time.

"There you go." She set her phone down on the little end table beside the wicker couch.

"Thanks."

"You're welcome."

They smiled at each other.

Blake tried to think of something to say. No need to go deep if they were better off light and friendly like this. He wouldn't drag some parts of his life into the present, and maybe she didn't want to talk about why she'd run out of the ER when her dad showed up.

They could get to that.

Her phone buzzed and moved across the table.

"The girls?" His stomach flipped over. What would his sisters think about him spending time with their friend?

"No." She stared at the screen. "It's one of the center kids. Apparently, Austin is there, smashing windows and threatening to set fire to it. I have to go over there."

Blake stood. "Then, let's go."

THIRTEEN

Destiny Reed dipped the mop into the bucket and hit the foot pedal.

"You should get out there and enjoy the party."

She glanced over at her boss, Conrad O'Connell. "I will. I'm almost done." She hit the mop on the floor with a satisfying *splat* and swished it back and forth. Her shift had been over for half an hour, but Conrad was still mad that she'd decided to go on an extended trip. He understood, except that he said he'd have to hire two people to replace her.

Destiny's shoulders ached. She'd dealt with everyone's shock and surprise over her decision, but the fact they were all so blindsided just proved how much they didn't bother to pay attention to her.

Merry Christmas to me.

As soon as the holidays were over, she was out of here. No more Benson—at least for a little while.

She needed the break. Not from Backdraft Bar and Grill. This place was great. And she loved her roommate and best friend...

The door swung open, and Conrad left, admitting Liam—nearly Conrad's body double. Not surprising since they were brothers.

Roxie squeezed between them and came over, grinning.

Destiny held out a hand. "Careful on the wet floor."

Roxie said, "You should've seen Tessa and River. They are *so cute*."

Liam clasped hands with Conrad, then stepped in while her boss headed out into the restaurant. They were closed, and all the food had been laid out on long tables for the friends and family Christmas party. "You're hiding in here."

Roxie gasped and spun around to him, her hands on her hips. "You weren't supposed to *say* that."

Liam's face pinked.

Destiny said, "I'm not hiding." Before Roxie could argue, she continued, "I'm taking a break."

"From people who care about you?"

Destiny didn't want to get into it. "Maybe they should care a little less." As if that was what she wanted. Or as if this was even about her family's reactions.

She hadn't told Roxie much about a certain police officer. She hadn't been able to voice the humiliation of unrequited feelings and had no intention of telling her sob story. She'd been an idiot. But that was years ago, right after he'd dumped his fiancée.

The night of shame.

Ugh. She didn't even want to think about it.

The morning after was humiliating, when she'd woken up with a hangover and realized what she'd said to him. The fact she'd actually kissed him—whether he liked it or not—in her drunken frustration. Okay, anger. And he'd politely extracted her from his personal space.

The next day she'd *vowed* to change her life. Four years and she was stronger in her faith than ever. "I'm not running away."

Roxie shot her a look.

"You and I have talked about it." And she'd thought she convinced Roxie that this wasn't about *him*. It was about Destiny doing what she felt God was leading her to do—regardless of that note in her that questioned if it wasn't at least a tiny bit about wondering if he'd notice her absence.

Liam said, "If you're trying to get his attention—"

"I'm doing what I feel God wants me to do." Destiny took a long breath, trying to calm down and not attack Liam with a dirty, wet mop. "This isn't a tantrum. I'm not acting out. Everyone needs to quit freaking out. If they're so worried, they can pray for me! At least that would be helpful."

"Good idea." Roxie stepped into the wet and held out her hand.

Destiny leaned the mop against the counter. The three of them held hands and stood in a circle while Roxie and then Liam prayed for her safety on her mission trip to Africa. For God to use her to touch the hearts of the sick children who lived in the home she would be working at.

A tear leaked from the corner of her eye.

Her friends kissed her cheek and left her with the mop.

Destiny sniffed back the warmth of her friends' care and concern, glad no one could see her being an emotional girl. Blake had never been able to handle their emotions. He'd sent the girls to her so she could manage whatever outburst they were having. The solutions usually boiled down to a nap, a bath, or a baked potato. Or chocolate, or ice cream. It depended on the sister.

"Why are you crying?"

That voice washed over her like the warm ocean. She'd been to Florida once, and that's what the warmth felt like.

But his tone? Total accusation.

Destiny turned, lifting her chin as she moved. He stood just inside the employee door like he had a right to come in that way like he owned the place. Like his father was some big shot state senator.

If he'd dumped the deputy mayor's daughter because she wasn't good enough for him, then some orphaned girl with a waitressing job wouldn't measure up.

Was she supposed to apologize for the fact she'd been drunk and angry and kissed him?

He wandered over with that loose stride. Off duty Jasper Hollingsworth wore nice fitting jeans, a dark green shirt, and a leather jacket. His ears were pink from the cold outside, but why wear a hat and squash the hairstyle he'd forged with gel?

She stood her ground, dressed in her food-stained work clothes. Black pants and a black T-shirt. Cheap white sneakers. Hair tied back. Makeup that had probably worn off hours ago. "Did you need something?"

He walked right into her space.

It was on the tip of her tongue to tell him to be careful of the wet floor.

But then, he was close. Way close.

"You're really leaving?"

She had to swallow first. "As soon as the holidays are over."

He leaned in. She could smell his cologne.

The door swung open. "Dest—whoa, sorry. Never mind."

Destiny closed her eyes. This was precisely when she needed one of the other servers to want her for something.

Jasper's lips touched hers.

Destiny's eyes flew open. Their lips nudged each other's, and his hand touched her cheek. She started a little at the cold. He should wear gloves.

Jasper pulled back, but he stayed close.

Was he going to tell her to "be careful" or "take care"? Was he going to ask her to stay?

"Merry Christmas, Destiny."

The door to the restaurant swished.

And he was gone.

FOURTEEN

"Thanks for driving, Blake."

He shoved his truck in park. "You're welcome, Let."

She spotted a flash of white teeth in the dark interior of the vehicle but couldn't stay here where she wanted to be—with him, just the two of them.

Instead, she shoved the door open while trying to focus on what was happening here. Rather than thinking about exchanging numbers with Blake, or how easy it felt to sit with him on the back porch and drink tea where it was warm. The cold remained at the edges—just like real life. But together, they'd been in a place that had been warm.

Basically, the opposite of her life growing up.

Her entire childhood had felt cold, like the air outside the truck.

She zipped up her jacket and tugged her gloves on as she passed a black-and-white squad car and headed for the center.

The front windows were shattered, leaving glass on the sidewalk. Her boots crunched over it, and she turned back.

Blake stood talking to a uniformed officer. He glanced over and nodded. "He's holed up inside."

Then it made sense why there was more than just one police car out here, even if they were unmarked. And an ambulance pulled around the corner at the end of the street.

Great. She loved a scene.

That must mean she was good to go in, so she stepped in the open front door. The huge wooden double doors stretched above her head; the lock on one door was busted and the wood beside it splintered.

A couple of cops stood at the end of the hall.

"You're Lettie?"

"Yes, I came with Detective Reed." She wasn't afraid of a positive association, and it seemed to help.

The officer lifted his chin. "Your friend locked himself in the office."

Violet winced. The center's director wasn't going to like that when he came back from his post holiday vacation. Then again, he only showed up every few months anyway, just to check if they were doing all right. He listened to their suggestions and left again, without doing anything to improve things. While he was gone, the volunteers got together and did what they decided would be best.

The officer's partner said, "He tore up the common room, smashed the game console, and broke a couple of chairs by throwing them out the windows. You'll need something to board them up with, and you'll need to call whoever has the insurance policy."

"And Mr. Phelps?"

The cop frowned. "The kid in there?"

"Yes."

"Talk him out, or we'll go in there and get him."

Violet said, "Thank you for waiting and giving me a chance to resolve this peacefully."

"You've got five minutes." The cop strode past her to the front door.

The partner patted her shoulder and shifted out of the way so that she had a clear shot at the office door. It was closed.

She twisted the handle and found it wasn't locked, but the door bumped something. A chair wedged under the handle.

"Who's there?" Austin sounded freaked.

"It's Lettie."

He didn't reply, but then she heard a chair scrape the floor. A few seconds later, he called out, "Come in."

Violet didn't want to be boxed into a small room with a volatile teen who could likely overpower her. The officer moved behind her, his weapon drawn.

She shot him a look, then eased the door open, staying by the frame. Leaning against it like all this was no big deal.

Austin sat behind the desk. Adrenaline had left his hands shaky, and sweat lined the hair at his brow. He'd run his hands through his hair a few times. Whatever had gotten into him that made him rage his way through the center, thankfully it had dissipated. He wasn't subdued, but she also didn't have to face the threat of him physically attacking her.

At least not without enough warning she could see it coming and react.

"Austin." She stuck her hands in her pockets, containing her personal space close to her where he couldn't reach it.

"Took you long enough to show up."

"If you wanted to talk to me, you could've called. The on-call staff member could've forwarded the call to my cell phone. We could've talked out whatever this is." Instead, he'd cost the center thousands in damage—if not more.

"Talk?" Austin snorted. He'd claimed the leather chair behind the desk. "You do that a lot. Doesn't seem to make much difference."

"Is this about the tribunal?"

"You think I care about that? Drew got his stuff back. Whatever." He shook his head, defiance in his features.

"The only way to figure this out is to keep talking." Not for him to take his anger out on furniture belonging to a nonprofit. "Sorry." She shrugged.

Either way, he was going to be arrested. If she had anything to do with it, she wouldn't have him charged in favor of giving him the chance to work off his debt by working here, doing maintenance and repairing what he'd broken.

What would Blake ask in this situation? She wanted to know what he'd suggest for repercussions. Not just because it would clue her in more to the kind of guy he was.

"You should be sorry. My brother is in jail because of you."

Violet frowned. "Because you asked me to look for him? That's not why he got arrested."

Austin got up and shoved the chair back. It hit the shelves behind the desk, and something toppled over to smash on the floor. "Yeah? It's not a coincidence. I asked you to look for Marco, and suddenly he's in jail, and you're hangin' with a cop." Austin continued by making a vulgar accusation about an exchange of favors.

She wasn't going to defend herself when it would only fall on deaf ears. "Your brother used a knife on a cop."

And dealers had been showing up dead, shot, and stabbed. Was Marco the one who'd been killing them? She'd pieced some things together. As far as she could tell from what Blake had said and what she'd heard around town, someone in Benson was taking out the competition. Trying to take over more territory and be the big drug supplier over all of it.

They were in the middle of a turf war.

But what did it have to do with Marco and his brother?

"All I did was go to see Marco's girlfriend. She said she hadn't seen him in weeks." Violet shrugged. "That was it."

He rounded the desk. "See? More talk."

Austin came at her.

The officer behind her said, "Watch it, bub."

"Yeah?" He shoved her, both palms open.

Violet stumbled back into the hallway.

"Hey!" The cop brushed past her and got into a struggle with Austin. More cops ran over and went into the room.

She could hear Austin yelling.

She turned and put her back to the wall, listening to the sound of screams and yelling and the thuds of the trouble-maker being subdued.

Stop fighting. You're only making this worse.

Her whole body shuddered.

"Hey, you okay, Violet?" Blake strode over. All goodness and confidence. The honorable cop who rearranged his life to take care of four younger sisters.

She shook her head, undeserving of his attention. A good man like him? He didn't know what he was getting with her. But it wasn't anything good.

Blake said, "Come here," and dragged her to him, wrapping his arms around her.

She cowered against him because being in his arms felt amazing. If only she could stay here, shrinking away from the rest of the world. Surrounded by his strength.

A sob worked its way up her throat.

"She okay?" someone asked.

Violet flinched. Sympathy was the worst. That look in a person's eye that said they cared, but you were also the biggest spectacle they'd ever seen—and it had been stop-and-stare worthy.

"Just get the kid out of here."

His voice rumbled against her cheek.

Violet held on to his waist.

After a while he finally said, "Are you okay?"

Violet straightened. "I thought I was okay, that it was done, but it all came rushing back."

Blake shifted, not letting go but moving enough that he could look down at her. "Tell me what it is."

She bit her lip.

Boots in the hall, a thunder of heavy footfalls on the floor headed toward them. "Blake!"

Saved by the arrival of his SWAT buddies.

FIFTEEN

"She just flipped out?"

Blake gripped the phone. "Yeah, Jas. That's what I said." He slammed the driver's door of his car and headed for the back entrance. But instead of going up to Intelligence this morning, he crossed the breezeway to the neighboring building where the morgue was housed in the basement.

"Why would she do that?"

"I figured, at first, she was mad at us—the cops there. Because we were arresting the kid."

"I still can't believe you let her go in there."

Blake said, "He wasn't dangerous."

"But he shoved her."

"Gutierrez said it was hard." Blake's stomach was still churning over it. He'd hardly eaten breakfast this morning after driving her home and leaving her in Doris's capable hands. He'd then gone home and tried to sleep, but it hadn't worked. He'd spent most of the night with his TV on and his laptop on the bed, looking up any related files from the fire department.

It helped to have an "in" with the brass of that branch of the FD. He'd called Trey—who'd replied to his text because he was up with the baby—and had him find all the callouts that ambulances had responded to with both a gunshot and a stabbing listed for the same patient.

They'd come up with only one. The responding paramedic? Violet Anderson.

It hadn't taken much digging to discover the man had died on the operating table. His body had never been claimed, so despite the fact the man had an ID and hadn't been listed as a John Doe, the guy remained in the morgue.

But not for much longer.

"She's getting under your skin," Jasper said. "You wanna forget everything, ignore all the reasons this is a bad idea, and sweep her up. Maybe take her to the beach...or a cabin."

Blake reached out to swipe with his key card but then let his hand drop. "Excuse me?"

"She does it for you."

He frowned. "What makes you say that?"

Jasper's laughter rang through the open phone line. "How about because in all the years we've worked together, you've never once talked about a woman the way you talk about her? You're worried about her *feelings*. This isn't about the case anymore. It hasn't been about the case since you saw her outside the bomber's house."

"Fine." His friend might have a point. Blake had spent at least ten minutes trying to decide whether to text her this morning or if he should let her rest.

"What you need to do is take her out."

"I don't need date ideas from you." He'd have to keep it in his pizza budget, not go broke trying to hit Jasper's valet parking ribeye standard.

"You didn't let me finish, bro," Jasper said. "You need to

get her talking. Get to know her. Get her to tell you what made her react like that and then convince her you'll make sure it never happens again. That she never needs to be scared."

Okay, so there was a lot to unpack in that statement.

Blake asked, "Who are you, and what have you done with Jasper Hollingsworth?"

"What? I can grow as a person."

Right. "Sure. Anyone can, but where did this come from?" Blake stepped aside for a couple of employees coming in for their workday. He nodded to both but only got a response from the older woman, a nod of acknowledgment. "What's going on with you?"

Jasper didn't talk right away. After a moment, he said, "Just thinking about stuff. Watching other people."

"Tessa and River?"

Jasper said, "It's not weird. I'm just...thinking about my thing. What happened, and who I was. I'm figuring some stuff out."

"And you think that what River did was convince her he could keep her safe?" Blake figured that was likely true, given what they had been through. Their relationship just worked. And for the first time in years, Tessa was in Benson for winter.

But it wasn't Jasper that'd been able to make her stay.

It was River, the guy she would probably end up marrying.

The situation was enough to make a grown man take stock of himself. "Some guys might not even care what that says about them, let alone make a change. You're a good man, Jas."

Jasper cleared his throat.

"What?"

"Ah, nothin'. I'm good. It's good."

Right.

"I should go. Breakfast with my dad." Jasper hung up before Blake could ask any more questions.

Blake swiped into the building and signed in at the morgue. The striking woman with a lab coat who admitted him to the morgue was very pregnant. "Good morning, Detective. I'm Doctor Carlton, but you can call me Sarah."

"He can call you Doctor Carlton."

Blake spun around and spotted a man on a stool in the corner of the room, his back to the wall. Every inch of the man's bearing was lethal, even the way he sat.

"That's my husband." Dr. Carlton smiled with the peaceful amusement of a woman who knew she was loved and safe down to her soul.

The man had a magazine in his hands but wasn't reading it.

Blake glanced between them.

"He's understandably nervous about the baby." Dr. Carlton laid a hand on her distended belly. "Which is, of course, completely normal for an expectant father. He wants to be close when the baby comes."

Okay, so there was more to it than that. But none of it was why Blake had come here. "You have an unclaimed body?"

She nodded and went to a table containing a body covered with a sheet. She folded the sheet back to reveal a deceased Caucasian male. "On occasion, despite the advances in medical life-saving techniques, it's impossible to save someone. This man's stab wound nicked his heart in a way that the surgeon couldn't repair."

"Was it George Anderson?"

She frowned and went to a tablet on the counter behind her. "Ah, no, I don't believe it was. One of his colleagues, Doctor Watts. Why do you ask?"

Blake tried to shrug it off. "Just curious."

A tiny noise came from the guy in the corner.

Dr. Carlton said, "The death was listed as a murder, given the man's injuries. I believe you have access to the case file."

Blake nodded. "The detective assigned went on vacation two days later, and the cop it was passed to didn't do much beyond pushing some papers around and making a phone call. This guy did seven years for assaulting a thirteen-year-old girl. I don't think anyone was all that motivated to punish whoever killed him."

"Justice should be blind, should it not?" she asked.

Another noise from the corner. Evidently, her husband didn't necessarily agree.

Blake could relate. "When you have to look the mother of that thirteen-year-old in the eye and tell her the man who destroyed her daughter got away with it, justice feels a little different," he said. "But that's why I'm a cop, not a district attorney. Or one of the scumbags who defend those guys."

The guy in the corner gave a dark chuckle. "What did you say your name was?"

He twisted his shoulders to look at the guy. "Blake Reed. Want my badge number?"

"I don't need it."

Dr. Carlton said, "Anyway, I've made you a copy of the files, and you're welcome to follow up if you have any further questions."

Blake shook her hand. "Thank you for your time."

He didn't try to shake the hand of the man in the corner. There was no need to be friendly with a man who had a lethality in him that surpassed even the craziest Vanguard employee. Who *was* this guy? The second he left, the guy would probably spend five minutes and find out everything about Blake. Who he was, who his family was. All the dirty secrets hidden in his closet.

A spot between his shoulder blades itched as he left. That odd feeling of being watched. Exposed. And yet, the man's wife had been at peace, secure in the fact he watched over her.

The kind of contentment River had given Tessa.

And all the other couples he'd seen meet and fall in love recently.

He didn't know Violet well, but he wanted to give her that peace and security. How could he give it to her if he didn't have it himself?

Dr. Carlton's husband could learn a lot about Blake's history. But not the worst of it...

Not the reason why Violet would never feel safe with him.

SIXTEEN

"I told them I'm not interested in pressing charges over a shove." Violet sipped the tea she'd made in the center's kitchen.

On the other side of the desk, behind the high-backed chair, the center's day manager nodded. Merry Chambers was blonde, wore no makeup, and hid her figure with clothes that seemed to have no shape. She constantly had her hair in a ponytail and loved to do the admin at the center while the other volunteers interacted more with the kids.

Violet didn't know her all that well, but Merry had never been anything but pleasant—even if she was quiet.

Merry said, "The board wants us to ask for the full restitution of damages."

"I get it." Someone had to pay for the repairs and replacement of the broken furniture. "Maybe we could have a fundraiser also."

"That's a great idea." Merry smiled, some of the worry over the manager's orders dissipating.

"I'll get out of your hair." She took Merry's empty mug for her and deposited both in the kitchen, in the dishwasher. She followed the bustle of noise and found Granny and her army of friends from the gym...or the library community group...or her game night group...or all the above...all sweeping, wiping, hauling trash out, and dusting.

Cold air blew through the gaps in the particleboard that the cops had come back with after the arrest. The devastation to the center had been a shock when she'd seen it this morning.

Blake hadn't wanted her to worry about it yesterday. He'd driven her home and told her that he'd secure the center.

After Austin had destroyed the place, the cops were the ones who'd stepped up and helped. And it wasn't just Blake. Evidently, a whole group of cops had shown up. Someone had donated the wood. The cops covered the broken windows and made sure no one could come in and loot the center. They'd swept the sidewalk outside, ensuring the damage didn't create a hazard for kids going to school.

It had been icy this morning. Add ice to that, and it could've been really dangerous.

As much as her heart broke that Austin had done it—and because he'd wanted to get back at her—the chance to see what kind of people the police in Benson were gave her more faith in people.

"Hey, girlie," Granny said as she used a broom to sweep under the coffee table and around the couches.

Violet looked around the room. Her eyes burned, and she felt the sting of tears gather.

All of them had dropped whatever they were doing today to be here to help a bunch of kids they didn't know. Kind of like the way Granny had moved houses to the townhome they now lived in and just about changed every part of her life to accommodate Violet living with her.

"You can just say thank you." Granny grinned. "No need to cry, even if we're doing a beautiful job."

"And looking good doing it," one of her cronies quipped.

Violet laughed, swiping away a tear. "I appreciate all of you."

One of them shrugged, her T-shirt slipping off one shoulder to reveal the strap of a sports bra. This physical labor was nothing for any of them, even though they were all at least seventy-five. Violet was a little intimidated by them. But mostly just because she wanted to *be* them when she grew up.

It wasn't hard to nurse some insecurities. But that wasn't why they did it.

"You're losing it."

Violet laughed. "Probably. I didn't sleep great. My head is all over the place."

Another one of them said, "When it should be firmly on that young man."

She blinked.

And yet another one said, "Speaking of firm young men…"

The first one wandered over to her friend. "I saw Russ Franklin at the coffee shop yesterday, not in his police commissioner suit. He always looks so uncomfortable in a monkey suit. No, he was in jeans. I had my Americano, and he walked by me. Mmm." She made a noise in her throat.

Violet had no interest in getting sucked into a conversation about Blake's boss's boss's boss or whoever. "We should figure out what else is left to tackle."

She cleared her throat, and Granny walked with her across the room.

"They don't have much fun in their lives." Granny handed Violet the broom. "When you're my age, you've got to get your jollies where you can find them."

"I don't think I want to know where you get yours."

Granny squeezed her cheek. "You don't have to worry about me, Let."

"I know." She sighed.

"You still thinking about it?"

She hadn't been for a minute, but now she was again. However, it was constantly at the back of her mind. Even if she moved across the world and never worked in anything related to the medical field, she'd still have the memory right there.

Her worst moment, ready to jump up and shame her into a spiral.

That's not what You want. Help me figure out how to let it go.

Granny eased onto a stool at the soda counter. "We all have things in our lives that we wish we could erase. Even your father."

As if he thought about that day the same way she did. "I doubt he regrets anything."

"Because you see only through your eyes." Granny's expression softened. "It's not a bad thing, and it's still influencing you. You're fighting your way through it."

"I should see it from his side?" No way. Not when it would only make her feel worse about herself. "Just so I can pretend he feels bad for how he reacted?" He probably didn't feel any regret whatsoever, as much as she might prefer him to be capable of empathy.

"People don't always want to push through the hard stuff they should think about."

Thinking about Blake would be a nice distraction. They'd exchanged numbers, but neither had sent a message since that initial contact.

Violet pulled out her phone now, wondering if she should touch base. But shouldn't he make the first move?

Did things still work that way? As if she had any practice dating. First, she'd been too busy. Then, she'd been taking pills to stay awake and drinking alcohol to get to sleep. Focused on being the best. After it all train-wrecked, she'd been putting her life back together and getting right with God.

Violet kissed her grandmother on the forehead. "Love you."

The older woman only chuckled. "I know, Let."

Violet wandered out to the hall, still cataloguing repairs that would need to be made. She noted a few things on her phone, then thumbed back to the thread that'd started with Blake.

She typed out a message asking how his day was going.

About to hit send, she pushed through the door to the basketball court. Someone grabbed her arm.

Her phone went flying across the floor.

Violet was forcibly spun around. She cried out as her chest and her cheek hit the wall. Whoever was behind her had a tight grip on her arm. He'd used her momentum against her and now stepped close. Smashing her against the wall.

She cried out again and tried to push back.

He only ground her harder against the wall.

Whoever it was, he was bigger and stronger than her.

"Strutting around, thinking you're everyone's savior."

Violet gasped as she fought to breathe.

"You're gonna give that boyfriend of yours a message." His voice was low and mean, his breath hot on her face. She didn't recognize his voice.

How could she? Her mind was a haze of desperation.

She still couldn't breathe.

A moan escaped her lips.

He made a noise in the back of his throat. Bile rose in

hers, and she fought to swallow it back while tears rolled down her face.

"You tell that cop boyfriend of yours that he steps up. He protects me and mine, or we tell everyone he's a killer."

She could only gasp while a million questions raced through her mind.

"Don't worry. He'll know exactly what I mean." He felt around, low by her hip.

Panic flashed in her mind like lightning.

"See you later, gorgeous." He pushed off her and backed off.

The release was so sudden her legs gave out, and she fell to the floor. Her head bounced off the basketball court. She blinked, her vision hazy as he swaggered away. Jeans. White T-shirt.

Consciousness swam in and out.

She tried to fight it, but the pain in her head eclipsed everything. She was about ready to give in and quit trying to stay awake when she heard a door open.

Someone screamed.

SEVENTEEN

The front doors to the emergency room slid open, and Blake ran in. He flashed his badge, and the desk nurse pointed down the hall. Blake found Doris Anderson in the hallway, wringing her hands together.

She must've heard him coming since she turned around.

"I got here as fast as I could."

Doris stepped toward him, shifting in a way that meant she needed a hug. He did have four sisters. Blake opened his arms, and she stepped into them. He held her in a gentle hug, looking at the door to the bay where Violet was likely being treated. A curtain had been pulled across the door, obscuring what was happening inside from view.

"Is she okay?"

Doris shook.

He eased her away and put his hands on her shoulders. "Why don't you tell me what's happened since you called me?"

She'd used Violet's phone, and Blake had answered, thinking he would get to speak with her about the night before and what'd happened. As soon as Doris told him about the attack, he'd jumped up from his desk and rushed to sign himself out.

"They brought her in, and the doctor said he needed to check her out. To see if she needed an MRI. She has a pretty big knot on her head." Doris winced. "She got a concussion a few years ago, so I've been praying that she hasn't knocked her head right back to that."

Blake nodded. He'd had a buddy who'd reinjured a previous concussion, and it was like the first time all over again. "I don't really pray much, but my sisters do. I can ask them to pray for Lettie."

"Honey bunches, you don't got nothin' if you don't got Jesus in you."

Blake grinned. "You sound like my sisters."

Doris grinned right back at him, though there was an edge of sadness in it. "Bring them over for Sunday lunch."

"I will." He eased close and gave her a quick hug.

He couldn't hear anything from inside the emergency room bay. He couldn't see anything through the curtain either, though he tried to peer in. Until he realized Violet might not be clothed if she was being medically checked out.

"Where is she?" The man's voice boomed down the hallway.

Doris muttered, "Here we go," under her breath and turned to meet Dr. George Anderson. He strode so fast down the hallway his white coat billowed behind him. Thunder on his face, in each footfall, and in the sound of his voice.

"Where is my daughter?"

Blake stepped in front of the door. The guy wasn't barging in there if Violet wasn't decent. Anyone could see through an open door. "Sir—"

"She's in there?" He looked like he was about to barge right through Blake.

Doris squared her shoulders. "George—"

"Don't start with me, Mother." He spun to face her. "This is your fault."

Blake flinched. "After the police interview your daughter about the man who assaulted her, they will be the ones to apprehend the culprit. Which I can assure you...is not your mother."

Dr. Anderson jerked his head around to stare at Blake. "Who are you?"

"We've met. But maybe you didn't notice someone other than yourself."

From Doris's expression, he didn't know if what he'd said was a good thing or if she just didn't appreciate his jab. But after the accusation Dr. Anderson had just thrown at his mother, there was no way Blake would let that go without saying something back.

"When I came down to sew up that cop?" Dr. Anderson shot a scathing look at Blake. "We may share skin color, but that doesn't mean you matter."

Doris turned to Blake, lifted a hand, and touched his cheek. "You matter very much."

She probably meant he mattered to Violet, but maybe also to her as well. Blake nodded. A tiny motion, all he could manage without flipping out.

"Big surprise," Dr. Anderson said. "You take in every wayward stray but have no time for your own son."

"I have all the time in the world for my son. It's that he doesn't have time for me." Doris lifted her chin.

Blake wanted to tug her to his side and put his arm around Doris's shoulders.

The door opened behind him. Dr. Anderson barked at the emergency room doctor who stepped out, a woman doctor not many years older than Violet's dad. But more mature, and the kind of woman who would never back down—not even to the chief of surgery.

"Doctor Anderson, I haven't had the pleasure in a few shifts. How are you?" She immediately turned to Doris. "Your granddaughter is resting. I ordered her something for the pain, and she needs to sleep. But I think we can avoid an MRI for now. Unless her status changes."

Dr. Anderson bristled. "I'm ordering an MRI."

"Because you believe I'm careless with my patients?" She practically looked down her nose at him. "I'm certain your attention to detail serves you well in the operating room, but this is my department."

Dr. Anderson swung around, lab coat swishing, and strode away.

The ER doctor sighed. Then she turned to Doris and offered her hand. Doris put hers into it, and the doctor said, "I assure you we're doing everything we can to help Violet recover."

"I know you are. Thank you." Doris nodded.

The doctor glanced at Blake. "Statement?"

"I'll make sure Violet gets the chance to talk when she's feeling up to it."

"Thank you, Officer."

Doris said, "He's a detective."

Blake's cheeks heated.

Then Doris asked, "How is her head?"

Blake squeezed her grandma's shoulder and slipped into Violet's room so he didn't hear private medical information. He eased the door closed behind him...and stopped.

She had her eyes closed. She was dressed in a hospital gown with one of those plastic ID bracelets on her wrist, and she was tucked into the sheets under the blankets. Dark circles were heavy under her eyes. She didn't seem to be sleeping, though.

Still, he didn't want to disturb her.

He turned to the door.

"Hey."

When he glanced back, she stared at him with pain-filled dark eyes. "Hey. I don't want to bother you if you're resting. I'll get your grandma to come and sit with you."

She lifted her fingers and motioned for him to move over to her.

Blake took her fingers in his hand. They were chilly compared with the room around her. He leaned against the side of the bed. "Did you see who did this? Did you get a good look at him?" He couldn't help asking. He was a cop, at least he'd been a cop for the better part of a decade.

He fixed things. He saved lives.

Then Violet's eyes filled with tears.

"I'm sorry. It's okay." His stomach flipped over. "Sorry."

"I didn't see him." She sniffed. "He shoved me against the wall." She shifted slightly on the bed, and pain flashed across her face. "He told me he had a message for you."

Blake flinched. "For me? What did he say?"

"He—*they*—want protection. Is it because of all those murder cases?"

"Maybe." Blake had to go easy. "Did he say anything else? Give you a way for me to find him?"

She shuddered. "My shorts." She waved at a cubby beside the desk. "Maybe."

This guy had touched her shorts?

She flexed her fingers.

Oh, he'd been squeezing too hard. "Sorry."

"Was my dad out there? I thought I heard him yelling."

"Don't worry about him." Blake wanted to ask her what

their deal was, but that could wait until later. Right now, she needed to heal, and he had some doors to kick in. First call? Jasper. His buddy would have his back.

And Doris would pray for them.

One way or another, they'd end this. Blake was going to make sure that happened. If what Violet said was correct—and he had no reason to believe it wasn't—then this happened because of him. It was his fault.

Violet blew out a slow breath.

He relaxed a little. "You need to sleep."

Her eyes fluttered closed. "He said..." Her words trailed off, then she continued, "He said you killed someone."

Blake shifted his fingers out from under hers. She opened her eyes, and all that pain was directed at him. "Will you come back later?"

He could only nod, manage to stumble to the door and out. "Doris, she would probably like to see you before she falls asleep."

He didn't even hang around long enough to hear her response. Outside, the winter air hit him full in the face and chilled the sweat on his forehead. He sucked in ice-cold breaths that stabbed at his throat. He put a hand to his chest and tried to calm down.

A low-slung black car rolled to the curb in front of him, pounding music. Two men in front, more in the back.

The back door opened, and someone called out, "Get in!"

EIGHTEEN

Two days and her head still ached, plus it kept waking her up at odd hours. She'd barely left the house and hadn't seen much sunshine. Granny had been tiptoeing around the house, keeping the lights dim.

Violet shuffled down the hall. Her hips ached where he'd ground her against the wall. That was probably the worst of the rest of her injuries. She had a minor scrape on one palm. Her jaw ached. The constant nagging pain wasn't easy to ignore.

She pressed her palm against the wall and stopped for a second.

Then she noticed a dark shape on the couch. What on earth...

That was far too big to be Granny. Violet had only gone from the bed to the bathroom and back for the past few days, not into the main living room. Who was sleeping on the couch?

She would regret it, but she reached out and slapped the light switch. She closed her eyes the split second before, and everything washed in bright illumination behind her eyelids.

Violet slowly opened her eyes long enough to see Blake sit up on the couch, blinking.

She turned off the light, flashes splitting the dark in front of her—resonant light her mind wanted to hold on to even though it hurt.

What was she supposed to think about him being on the couch? He wasn't breaking in or sneaking around. He'd been asleep.

Now he stood up, very much awake. And she had the distinct impression of his bare torso stamped in her mind.

Blake Reed, Mr. Hotness Police Detective, came to stand in front of her. He touched her elbow. "You okay?"

"I just came out to get a different drink." She'd drank so much water over the past few days she was sick of it.

"Can't sleep?"

She sighed. "I feel like I've slept too much."

"Come on." His fingers slid down her arm and wrapped in hers. "I'll make you the drink I'd make for the girls when they couldn't sleep."

She slid onto a stool while he turned on the soft yellow light over the oven. "Thanks. You're a good brother."

He looked over, the fridge door open. He raised one brow at her, which gave him a sensual look, not at all like a brother. "You get that's not why I'm here, right?"

Her head hurt way too much for this. "I have no idea why you're on my couch in the middle of the night."

He put the half gallon of milk on the counter and came over. "Just so it's clear." Blake eased near to her and touched his lips to hers. "I may have practice as a big brother, but I feel something different with you. Okay?"

Violet blinked. "O-kay."

"Now, I'll make you my nightie-night drink. That's what Hope always called it."

Violet smiled. Of course, she would. The girl had funny names for nearly everything. "She's a good kid."

"The best. They all are."

Violet sighed. "I have no siblings."

He set a mug in the microwave. "I want to hear about your life growing up and your family, but I also need to talk to you about something."

Like where he'd been the last couple of days? He'd left the hospital abruptly. "I didn't believe it when that guy told me you killed someone." Not then, and not since. "I just wish I could've seen his face. Given something more than 'I don't know' in answer to the officer's questions."

He slid a mug in front of her and then stayed close behind her. His chest warmed her back. She leaned her head back on his shoulder, and Blake pulled her back into a loose hug.

Then she took a sip of the drink.

"What is this?" It was warm, sweet, and creamy.

"It's just milk and some sugar."

Violet groaned. "It tastes amazing. Why does it taste amazing?"

She felt him chuckle against her back.

"Tell me whatever you have to tell me." She waved to the other stool.

Blake eased onto it, turned toward her so that one knee cocooned her in, and the other foot rested on the rung of her stool.

She would've been interested in how close he chose to sit at any time other than two in the morning when her pain pill hadn't kicked in yet.

He ran a hand up and down her back. "I'm glad you're feeling better. I was worried."

"I always bounce back eventually."

"Did you see your father in the hospital?"

Not what she wanted to talk about, but she'd have to explain it at some point. Probably sooner, not later. "You're stalling."

She was deflecting in the same way, but that wasn't the point.

Blake eased around so they were shoulder to shoulder. So he didn't have to look her in the eye?

"It wasn't anything you did or didn't do that got you hurt. It was because of me and the fact they wanted to hit me where it hurt by hurting you. I'm sorry."

"You don't need to apologize."

He shook his head. "It's my fault that—"

"My dad always says you should *never* apologize for *anything*." His voice proclaimed it in her head, the same way so many other things circled like a refrain in her mind. "I disagree with it. For the last few years, I've been trying to relearn a lot of what he taught me. Learning to say you're sorry is hard. But you don't have to apologize for this. You're not responsible for someone else's actions, Blake. You can't control what people do."

He let out a long breath. He'd been really worried about her reaction. "I still don't like that you were targeted because of your association with me."

"Better than being lonely."

Out the corner of her eye, she saw him turn to her. Even with many people in her life and living with her grandmother, she still wanted more—like the close connection of a relationship.

"I thought I had what I needed with SWAT." He cleared his throat. "We worked together for years and became a solid team that hung out after shifts and on holidays and weekends. Then things started to change. The lieutenant got married, and Dakota had to leave to find a better footing. Liam is with

Roxie now, and the team was moved to part-time. So, I'm in Intelligence, and Jasper works white-collar crimes."

She held the mug with both hands, sipped, and took the time to catalog the shift in his expression. He didn't seem like the kind of guy who let many people below the surface, yet he'd found it with SWAT.

"Lately, everything feels like it's changing."

"Like you're standing on shifting sand."

He nodded. "The girls told me to pray, but I'm not sure God would listen."

She could've jumped to say, *Of course, He would*, but something held her back. "I thought that as well. I hit rock bottom. Pills to keep me awake, alcohol to help me sleep. I put so much pressure on myself, and I didn't even realize how hard I was pushing to become a doctor. The best doctor. Better than my father. Perfect at everything. A spotless record."

And then it all came crashing down.

"At my worst, at my absolute lowest, when I had nothing and God by all rights should never have listened to me, He did."

Blake set both forearms on the breakfast bar and hung his head.

No need to push him too far too fast and have him shut down. She would rather plant a seed and pray God helped it grow.

The way Granny had with Violet.

For years.

Please don't let this take years, Lord. For Blake's salvation, not just because she didn't want to have to wait that long to have a relationship based on the solid footing of two people resting in Jesus.

She asked, "So, why were you sleeping on my couch? I

mean, I've fallen asleep on it enough times watching a movie. It's a nice couch."

Blake lifted his head. "Nicer than mine. I'll have to come here and watch basketball in the future. And football. And baseball. I'm equal opportunity."

"A sports guy."

"In need of a comfy couch." He turned to her, a sappy look on his face. "Just a sporting match a day can help a poor lost soul in need."

Violet shoved at his shoulder, laughing.

"But seriously, I want you and Doris to be safe. She agreed she'd feel better if I was here at night."

"And how long is that going to last?" He couldn't possibly stay here indefinitely.

"I'm not going to let anything happen to you, Lettie." His warm palm settled on her back. "I promise."

There was more than guilt in his expression. She saw determination there as well.

And a healthy dose of fear.

What was he so afraid of?

NINETEEN

Detective Wilks eased into his chair across from Blake early the following day, moaning extra loud.

Blake glanced over from the report he'd been typing up on his computer. "You okay over there?"

"Days of surveillance. Days in the front seat of a car."

"Doesn't sound fun."

Wilks groaned, then reached into the inside of his jacket and dribbled liquid from a metal flask into his coffee cup.

Blake pretended not to have noticed. This guy would be retired soon, and Blake had enough enemies. He was sleeping on a couch, not exactly hours spent in a car—but not a cushy detail.

"He hasn't shown anywhere. Not that any of us even know what to look for." Wilks powered on his PC. "A dead guy, I guess."

Meanwhile, someone was murdering dealers, which was why some of the other dealers wanted Blake to protect them, or they'd tell everyone that he had killed someone.

Wilks said, "Sure you didn't miss something in that house? Maybe there was another guy hiding like the one in the freezer that your drone missed." The man's tone was sarcastic.

"The lining of the freezer meant the drone's heat sensor didn't pick up anything."

"Sure. If you say so."

"We searched the whole house. There was no other DNA found except the renter—"

"A guy who's been dead for years."

"And a couple of other unidentified small samples." One would likely come back as a match to Marco at least. The other? Maybe the victim Marco had heard in the area near the freezer.

DNA testing could take weeks. Only the rush put on that initial sample got them a result so fast in ID'ing the bomber. No one expected it to come back as a guy declared legally dead years ago by a distant family member. Probably someone looking to inherit his belongings—or property, or the contents of his bank accounts.

Some guy, long dead. A soldier in Desert Storm who'd come back in one piece, and not long after, he'd never been heard from again.

"Reed!"

He twisted around in his chair at the sergeant's call. "Yes, ma'am?"

"Your report is taking too long. What's the scoop on the meet?"

He'd gone right from the hospital into a car, and then he'd been whisked across town to an empty warehouse. Inside were scattered pallets and patches of snow from where the roof leaked. He'd huddled in his winter coat while a couple of dealers explained what they wanted from him.

The same crew who'd paid the attacker to hurt Violet.

He'd been about ready to empty his clip into the whole

group, but thankfully, logic had filtered to the surface, and reason took over. He'd stayed his hand and decided following through with the meeting as a cop would serve him best.

And Violet.

And justice.

Not to mention the expectations his sisters had for who they wanted him to be.

Out of respect for them, he didn't kill in the name of revenge. He only listened to them.

Blake hit print on the report and got up, locking the profile on his computer after the page had come out. He took the paper to Deerdan's office and stood just inside the door. "Near as I can tell, only a few dealers left in Benson haven't been hit."

Deerdan said, "That is, if this guy doesn't move on to the lower-level dealers after he's done with the higher-ups supplying everyone else."

Hopefully, this wouldn't continue for that long. "They want protection when they go out. I got the feeling there's something big coming up, so I'll be sticking close for the time being. Trying to get a handle on what it is."

"Good." She nodded. "If we know what's coming, we can set up, catch them in the middle of a buy or payment, and take them all down. If our murderer shows up along the way, we'll get him, too."

"That was also my thinking." Even if he didn't like the cavalier way she said it.

"We're spread thin right now, so call if you need backup."

"I'll be doing it solo for now. They don't want me bringing along anyone else."

Deerdan said, "Because you're the one they think they can press if things go wrong. That you'll fold under the pressure of being outed for… What did they say they had over you?"

"Murder."

She snorted. "I've read your file. And I know who your father is, but we don't get to choose where we come from. Any idea what they're referring to?"

Yes. "Who knows what they believe, and who told it to them?" He'd like answers to both of those questions.

"You're the guy they think they can extort for what they want, but that's the thing."

Blake asked, "What is?"

"Risky move on their part. Bringing a cop into their business." Deerdan sat back in her chair.

"They're scared." That much was evident without any of them saying so. "And what they need is worth more than the risk."

"That's it exactly." She nodded. "What worries me is the other case and what a bomber might do to hit back at us now that he's aware we're hunting him."

Blake blinked at the sudden shift. She didn't think the murdered dealers and the bombing cases were connected, did she? He hadn't seen any indication they were linked so far. "Have we been able to nail down any business partners, family connections, or other known associates?"

She shook her head. "The guy was a ghost, before and after he went missing. We've got nothing."

"Except the fact he isn't dead. And Marco said he's *not* the man Marco met in that house."

"Exactly," Deerdan said. "Marco made a deal in exchange for an artist sketch of the guy. We get an eyewitness image, maybe the best we're gonna get, and he's out on very little bail."

Marco was back on the streets, pending his trial. "I hope

he stays one step ahead of this. Maybe he'll be smart and split town."

"As long as he's back for his court date, I don't care."

Blake's focus had to be the dealers, and what would amount to an undercover case. Except that the role he was playing was that of Blake Reed, police detective. He hadn't decided if he was going to pretend to be on the take. After all, he had no idea if they knew about what happened when he was fourteen, or if this whole "murderer" thing was about something far more recent.

He needed to know what information was on the streets about him.

What reputation did he have?

It would fall back on Violet, the way this business with the dealers had. He would do what he could to keep her safe. But the threat of him being discredited was far more likely. She could lose all her standing in the community as a first responder and as someone who helped kids.

"Focus on the ones who reached out. If they're scared, they'll let too much slip out." Deerdan shifted her focus to her computer. "Stay safe, Detective."

"Yes, ma'am."

"And if you need backup, put in a request for someone who will..." She glanced at him. "Blend in."

He nodded. "I know a couple of guys who'd fit."

"That'll be all."

Blake left the report on her desk and trailed out. Wilks pecked the keyboard at his computer with two fingers. He was writing up a report about surveillance that delivered nothing.

Not Blake's favorite, sitting for hours and accomplishing nothing as a result. He'd rather be up and moving, working a case.

Not protecting dealers so they weren't murdered. So they could be safe to keep breaking the law.

He pushed out a sigh. Almost tempted to pray for a result that meant he could slap cuffs on these guys *and* manage to keep the truth from becoming common knowledge. Almost. Something kept him from voicing the words—even in his mind.

God didn't listen to guys like him.

No matter what the girls said.

Until the threat was over, he needed to keep things where they were now and make sure they didn't get in deeper. Even though he was ready to jump right in and ask Violet more of her story. Get something going between them.

Things would be sticky with her being connected to the case. He couldn't make it public and official. Especially when he was unofficially protecting her.

His phone rang, so he dug it out of his pocket. The number for his dad's prison. He swiped the screen to answer. "Detective Reed." He headed for a quiet alcove.

"I saw the morning paper."

Blake stepped into the empty break room and saw a newspaper on the table. He laid it flat and stared at the bomber's photo above the headline about a local man the police believed was back from the dead. "Something I should know?"

"Too many ears."

The line went dead.

Blake stared at the phone. What was that about?

TWENTY

Violet settled into the passenger's side of the car, an oddly clean and not quite brand-new SUV. Jasper rounded the front and got in the driver's seat.

"Thanks for being my babysitter while Blake is working."

Jasper grinned at her. "You're saying that because I didn't tell you what we're doing yet."

"Oh, no. What? What did you get me into?"

He laughed and pulled away from the curb in front of the town house. She turned and waved at Granny.

Jasper asked, "Sure you're able to be out and about?"

"I slept great." After she'd finished the sweet milk Blake had made her. "But I'll crash later and take a big nap."

"All right, sounds good."

"So, where are we going? And whose car is this? It doesn't seem like something you'd drive." He was more of a loafers and BMW kind of guy. Except right now, he was dressed in worn jeans over beat-up tennis shoes, a dark blue Henley, and a brown jacket. "Are we going somewhere undercover?"

He hadn't told her what occasion to dress for.

Jasper held out his hand. "Chill, we're not going under-cover. This is my car, or one of them anyway."

If he wasn't the son of a wealthy state senator, she'd think he was on the take. "Okay. So, what are we doing?"

"My mother started a nonprofit that prepares food boxes for low-income households. I work there when I'm not on shift, and we have some deliveries to make."

Violet stared at him.

He pulled up to a red light and glanced at her. "What?"

"Nothing." No one who knew him had told her this. Maybe no one in his life knew the extent of the things he cared about.

"Don't tell anyone, okay?"

"If Blake asks what we did, I'm not going to lie. But I'll do my best not to betray your confidence."

All he said was, "Four stops, lunch, then home in time for your nap."

Violet said, "Thanks for letting me come with you. I needed to get out of the house."

"You can help carry some of the lighter things." He pulled into an apartment complex on the rougher side of town and navigated the cracked asphalt of the parking lot, where he eased into a visitor spot. They knocked and dropped off boxes to two different homes. One was a woman who looked to be running a home daycare, given the logo on her shirt and the worn exhaustion behind her smile. The other was an older Asian man, and Jasper had surprised her again by using a few phrases in Japanese.

When they got back in the car, she asked, "Do you speak any other languages?"

His jaw tightened. "My father said Spanish was beneath us. Can you believe that?"

"So you didn't vote for him."

Jasper barked a laugh. "You have no idea how relieved I am that he got into office before I could vote."

"And now, whenever he's up for re-election?"

"What I write on my ballot is no one's business but mine," he said.

"How refreshing." It seemed like everyone was determined to convince those who disagreed to come around to their side. It should be an individual choice based on far more factors than just the popularity contest it typically became.

"But you didn't come with me to talk politics. And I've declared my life a baloney-free zone."

She laughed, and it made her head hurt, but it felt good. "Good policy." Did that mean if she asked him if there was a woman in his life, he'd be honest?

Jasper cleared his throat. "Do you know if Blake has heard anything about how Destiny is doing in Africa?"

She heard the note of something desperate in his voice. Destiny meant more to him than he wanted to admit. And he couldn't ask Blake how his sister was doing. "I haven't heard an update. I emailed her myself just to tell her I was praying for her. But I'm not expecting a reply."

He parked in front of the complex where Marco's girlfriend lived, far from the door, but the street had cars on both sides. He pulled up super close behind a blue Toyota. "We won't be long, but let's not block this person in any more than we need to."

That was probably her cue to get the last bag of paper goods while he got the box of dry foods and two bags of perishables.

On the second floor, he turned left.

She stopped at Marco's girlfriend's apartment. "I'm just going to knock while you deliver that." She hooked the bag on his two fingers.

After the second knock, she gave up. Marco's girlfriend wasn't home.

Jasper spoke to the delivery recipient at the end of the hall, then wandered back to her. Did anyone in his life know this side of him? If only she could take a photo of this version of Jasper and send it to Destiny. Overstepping, probably, but the people who cared about him would see their faith in him was valid.

She could relate to his struggle. Her father had taught her to earn every inch of respect she gained through sweat equity. His was probably just as demanding of him.

Both of them had been twisted in knots and grew up with issues from that treatment. No one's parents were perfect, that was for sure. But both her father and Jasper's were the same kind of father—one who expected nothing but blind obedience as they rose to the lofty heights their fathers demanded they achieve.

They took a side door out since it was closer to the car. Halfway down the path, Jasper touched the small of her back. "Stay close." His gun was in his hand.

She looked around. "What is it?"

"Over by the dumpster."

They were headed in that direction. She spotted what he had. "Is that shoes?"

"With feet in them. There's someone lying on the far side."

She picked up her pace, and he stuck with her. "They're not moving."

Jasper had her stand to the side. "Don't move." He gave her his phone. "Call 911."

But her emergency medical training kicked in. And she knew this man. "It's Marco." She crouched by his side and felt for a pulse. Then she leaned down and listened to his mouth.

"He's alive. He's been shot, and there's another wound." From a knife, maybe.

Jasper spoke into his phone. She held her sweater over the worst of Marco's bleeding wounds.

Three minutes later, the ambulance rolled to a stop at the curb, followed by a black-and-white police car. She recounted her assessment to the responding EMTs and got out of their way.

They whisked Marco to their stretcher and into the back of their ambulance. With lights and sirens flashing, they took off.

"That was fast."

She rubbed the back of her hand across her forehead. "No time to lose. I'm glad we didn't find him when it was too late."

Jasper nodded. "Me, too."

Another few police cars pulled up, including an unmarked one. Blake climbed out. Spectators had started to gather, and a CSU truck pulled up.

The technician lugged a case with her. "Morning."

She looked like she was about to introduce herself, but a uniformed officer jogged up. "Detective Hollingsworth, your car's blocking a lady in."

Jasper tossed his keys. "Put the seat back after you move it."

"Sure." The officer looked a bit in awe.

"Thanks."

Blake came to Violet and hugged her. She kept it brief even though she didn't want to. She was unable to keep from thinking about their conversation in the middle of the night. Did he remember also?

"Doing okay?"

She nodded. "I'm good."

They told him about finding Marco by the dumpster.

Violet said, "This is where his girlfriend lives, but she didn't answer her door. I was going to say hi."

Jasper scratched his jaw. "Maybe Marco came here to see if she could help him treat his wounds. Didn't get far enough. Or he was hit on the way across the courtyard to the door."

A thunderous crack echoed through the air between the building and the trees, bouncing back while fire erupted into a ball above where they'd parked.

Jasper's car flipped up and back, somersaulting in the air.

Violet gasped. She was spun around and thrown to the ground. Blake landed on top of her. He'd tackled her to the ground.

His face stopped close to hers, their noses touching.

Smoke filled the air around them.

Jasper yelled, "My car!"

She looked over and saw his face crumble.

"That officer was inside."

TWENTY-ONE

Blake shifted off Violet, tugging her up with him. "You okay? Did you hit your head?"

Maybe tackling her wasn't the best idea, but he'd reacted without thinking. Had she hit her head on the ground? Another concussion was the last thing she needed right now.

She laid a hand on his arm. "I'm good. Thank you."

At least that was one thing he didn't have to worry about right now. The rest of his life felt like a powder keg ready to blow...no pun intended. His father's words were still running through his head. Blake had checked the morning paper, and the front page had been about the bomber being at large. They'd mentioned the guy whose DNA was in the house. Was that what his dad wanted to talk about, but he couldn't because he had no privacy in prison?

"Are you okay?"

He blinked and focused on her. They were both on their feet now. Blake managed to nod. "I'm okay."

She cared. If he could trust that expression on her face. The woman in front of him had been through a rough few days, but she was a good person. He'd always thought that good people should have an easier time in life. It didn't work out that way, though.

She had the same kind of peace in her that his sisters did. And her Granny.

Sirens drew his attention. Violet stood close by his side, sliding her arm around his waist while he watched the fire truck turn the corner. Lights and sirens going.

The car had landed upside down, and flames were licking up into the sky.

Thankfully, Marco had been taken away already. But they might need another ambulance here. Or the coroner.

"He was in the car. He was moving it for Jasper."

Blake kissed her forehead. "Let's move closer. But we don't want to be in their way."

The firefighters jumped out and got their gear, working in formation with minimal instructions from their captain. Blake recognized the guy and lifted his chin.

Jasper stood on the far side of the destroyed car talking to a civilian, an older gentleman.

The captain headed for Blake and Violet. "You both okay?" His attention shifted to Violet. "Do you need an ambulance?"

She shook her head. "I'm okay. Most of these injuries are from a few days ago."

True, but she could use a checkup with a doctor. He'd ask her later. Captain Julio Espinoza-Vasquez was a guy he'd played basketball with, a former wildlands hotshot in Alaska who'd come home and ranked up with the local fire department.

Blake stuck his hand out, and Espinoza shook it. "There was someone in the car when it blew. One of ours. A uniformed patrol officer."

Espinoza's glove left a layer of grit on Blake's hand. His expression shuttered. "Do I need to worry about any other explosives?"

As a captain, he could absorb the shock of losing a brother in the PD, but he had to coordinate his team as well. Ensure the safety of his men for the duration of this callout.

Blake wiped his hand on the leg of his jeans, not that those were much cleaner than Espinoza's gloves. "I don't believe so." He turned to Violet. "Did you see anyone around the car?"

She shook her head. "We were inside, then helping Marco."

"So someone had time to plant the explosives while you were occupied?"

She nodded. Jasper was probably asking bystanders the same questions.

Espinoza said, "Under the driver's seat would be my guess. Your guy probably never had a shot."

Violet sniffed. "Who would do that?"

"Jasper's dad is going to put two and two together and think Hollingsworth is in danger." And the last time that'd happened, Jasper got put on lockdown and had to be on indefinite suspension until the captain convinced his father that the threat was over. The senator's will always trumped Jasper's ability to do for himself.

This could turn out to be a nightmare for Jasper, but wasn't worse than what this officer's family would go through.

Everything was spinning out of control. Keeping it all contained and keeping the threads of these cases straight was getting difficult.

Violet would be praying once she got through the shock. His sisters would do the same when they found out.

His alternative, if he even wanted to change his MO, was

to look into the faith they all shared and see if it could help him. But that meant having faith in God that things would still turn out okay even if He was in charge.

After years of running his own life the way he wanted, giving up control didn't sound all that inviting.

"Cap!"

Espinoza turned to his firefighter.

"Flames are out. We need the ME or the coroner."

And Blake needed to get Violet out of here so she didn't have to see this police officer's charred body every time she closed her eyes. The first responders would absorb that blow for her—and everyone else who didn't do a job like this.

"Come on." He tugged her away from the scene, nodding to Captain Espinoza.

Jasper met them by the car. "Are you taking Violet to the hospital?"

She stiffened. "No. I don't need to see a doctor."

Jasper's eyes widened.

Did she mean she didn't want to see a particular doctor? Blake said, "We can hit an urgent care or your primary physician?"

She shook her head, but it looked like it hurt. "I'm okay. I just need to rest. I didn't hit anything."

"I'll drive you home. I can take your statement there." Then he'd have to get back to work and write up his own report about this. Someone would have to investigate the bombing.

If it turned out to be connected to his father, it would look suspicious if that was Blake.

Good thing he had all the cases he could handle right now.

He glanced at Jasper. "You good, Jas?"

His friend stuck out his hand. "Keep her safe."

They shook, and Blake slid into the driver's seat. He put

the key in, and Violet gasped. She grabbed his forearm. "Don't turn it on! That's what the officer did!"

Blake didn't shift in the seat, even though he wanted to turn to her. He let go of the key and bent around the steering wheel to look under his seat. "Hand me a flashlight."

She gave him her phone with the camera light on.

"Nothing down here but old fries and a business card I lost." He straightened. "We're good."

She bit her lip.

Blake turned the engine on. He pulled out and headed toward the main street. "Might be a good idea to see your doctor—"

"No."

Blake held his reaction back. That was emphatic. Maybe she'd used up her ability to soften anything, and this was maxed out Violet, who'd seen something horrible and was at the end of her tether.

He drove to her town house and parked out front.

"Thanks. I don't want to know how long it would've taken me to get back in a car if you hadn't been here. I don't think I want to be the driver for..."

Blake turned to her and saw the glaze of fear in her eyes. He touched her cheek. "It's understandable."

"I need to call Dennis." She blew out a long breath.

"Who is that?"

"You know him. Captain McCauley. He's my sponsor."

Blake's eyebrows rose. "Captain McCauley is your sponsor?"

She nodded.

"Wow, that's awesome."

Her face crumpled the way the girls' did right before they started crying. He was already tugging her over. "C'mere."

She dissolved against him.

Blake rode out the storm, unlocking her seat belt so she wasn't all tangled and getting a couple of napkins from the glove box.

"You're pretty good at that." She shifted away. "Guess it's all the sisters."

He smiled because it was true. "I'm glad you have someone to call."

"Maybe he'll give me an inside scoop on how the case is progressing. I don't want to be around another bomb."

"He tells you?"

She snorted, then blew her nose. "No, he does not." She wiped her nose another time. "It's very annoying. I could hear juicy stories, but it's like he only wants to hear about how I'm doing."

"I can tell you plenty of juicy stories."

She grinned. "Can you come in, or do you have to get back to work?"

"I can come by as soon as I'm done with my shift. I can bring dinner if you want?" Which would lead to them spending more time together. "I have a thing late tonight, but I'm free before it."

"Okay, guess I'll face Granny alone." She grinned, apparently better now that she'd taken some time to process her adrenaline-fueled emotions.

"Blake?"

"Yeah, Let?"

She bit her lip. "Was the bomb meant for Jasper, or me? Am I in danger?"

TWENTY-TWO

"Anything else?"

Violet leaned her head back on the couch. "I think that's all of it."

Instead of answering her question about whether she was in danger, he'd given her a hug because he honestly didn't know. Then he'd walked her inside and taken her statement. Talking through it had the effect of allowing her to see the morning's events after the fact, without the shock. She still shivered with the lingering fear and surprise.

"Here." He tugged over the blanket she used when there was a chill in the air.

"Thanks." Violet settled under it, tucking it around her, when she'd honestly rather be in his arms again. Except that would lead to them both being distracted.

Especially with their emotions all over the place. Things could get risky, and he had a shift to get back to. She needed some tea and a chance to settle her nerves.

"Given what you've told me, I can't say if you were the target or Jasper. Or they're targeting you to get to me."

She studied his face. In their last conversation, he'd been

honest about the guilt that came from her being hurt because of him. "So, we have no idea why the car exploded?"

Blake said, "The *why* is because someone wanted to take a life. Probably to get our attention."

Violet blinked back tears. A man was dead, and her mind wanted to settle on being glad it wasn't her. But that wasn't fair to the family who'd lost their son—or brother. Had someone lost a husband? "Was he married...that officer?"

Blake's expression softened. "For now, just focus on resting. Later, I'll find out anything you want to know about him. And if you want to go to the funeral, I'll take you."

"Thanks." He did so much. Steady and calm.

She needed to hug all his sisters and say thank you. What guy knew how to handle a distraught woman the way Blake did? He would be a catch for any woman.

She wanted to be the one.

Is it him, Lord? Is he the one?

No matter what her heart wanted, it had to be a God-thing.

Blake's brows drew together, and his expression became a little lighter. "What are you thinking about?"

"Uh." She had to cough. "I don't think you want to know."

Not just her crying spell, but he also handled the death of another police officer with calm.

"How do you do it?"

Blake sat back on the armchair. "Do what?"

"A cop died today."

"It'll hit me. Probably in the shower, where I can pretend that it's all just water and not that I'm crying over a man I barely knew," Blake said. "I can't ignore it. Like anyone, I have to feel it rather than bury it, or I'm not helping myself."

Violet nodded. "I know that. I've lived it." She glanced down, looking at the shift of the blanket as she ran her fingers over the knee of her jeans underneath. "That's what landed me in an EMT job with a police captain as my sponsor. Though, he's only Dennis to me."

"I'd like to hear the story," Blake said quietly.

"I'd rather never tell it again." But that wouldn't help her have healthy, deep relationships. If she was going to get close to Blake, it meant being honest about who she was and where she'd been in her life. "I can blame it on my father, but that would be far too easy. I can tell you all about how he pushed me and pushed me. He never let me do anything without being the best or the fastest. The first. The one with the highest score."

"Sounds like Jasper's dad."

Violet nodded. "And given our zip code, they're similar in multiple ways."

"Silver spoon?"

"I gave it up voluntarily. But not just because I lost my job, I still have the student loans to pay off, and I live with Granny."

Blake stayed quiet and didn't move.

"I knew the risk when I took what I thought I needed to take to stay awake studying. I knew the risk of not eating and using alcohol to check out enough to get the bare minimum of rest. When I hit rock bottom, I was twenty-five pounds lighter than I am now."

He winced.

"Yeah, not healthy." Even if she didn't love *all* of her current curves. "He pushed me to medical school, and I could've done it. I could've been chief of surgery—or whatever department I wanted—and I'd have reached it at a younger age than he did."

And she'd have hated who she became.

Because she'd have been exactly like her father.

"But I hit a wall. Crashed and burned. *Hard.* I had some kind of crazy nervous breakdown in the middle of a shift. All the residents around the bed of this kid... A burn victim. I couldn't even look at her. My heart felt like it was going to explode out of my chest.

"My father just stood there talking like she wasn't even human. Like the lifelong journey this girl would go on meant nothing to him. All that mattered was the correct answer to what medication she needed next and what complications we needed to watch for.

"When I wasn't the first one to answer, you should've seen the look he gave me." Violet managed to swallow. "He grabbed my elbow and dragged me into an alcove. Started berating me about shaping up and doing better."

She didn't look at Blake. She was so far back in her memories that all she could see was her father's face in her mind.

"He was shaking he was so furious. And then I threw my notebook at him. It hit him right between the eyes. Then I just...lost it. I flew at him, screaming. Hitting him. Kicking him. It was like I wasn't even me." She pulled in a shuddering breath. "Someone called security. They dragged me off him and held me down."

"Did he call the police?"

"He never pressed charges. I think he was too embarrassed." She sniffed. "But it was Sergeant McCauley that showed up. Took one look at the state of me and realized I didn't need a psych ward—which was what my father wanted. He got me into a two-week rehab program and didn't let me do anything without checking with him first. Granny was there when I left, and the two of them figured everything out."

She'd been attending meetings regularly ever since. Every day at first, and now every few weeks or every month when she needed it.

"They prayed for me, then with me. All the ups and downs of recovery and making amends. Finding a new job, much to dad's embarrassment that I'm a lowly paramedic."

Her dad hadn't reacted well at all when she'd tried to apologize to him.

He'd practically thrown her out of the office.

Her stomach roiled a bit, but overall, she didn't feel too bad. Now Blake knew it all. Her sordid history and her biggest failure.

Maybe he didn't want to take on her and all her baggage.

Maybe he thought she should be more than a paramedic like her father.

"You've come through a lot, and you're still standing."

Violet stared at him.

"I've seen people fold when faced with a lot less. In my job, I see the other side. What happens when someone refuses to accept the hand that reaches out to them? Or they have no one to offer them help."

She nodded. "That's why I help out at the center." And why she tried to talk to some of the patients she helped in the ambulance, handing out cards for the rehab place she'd been to.

Everyone had to make the choice between avoiding their own issues or dumping the fear so they could stop hiding.

"And it's why I separate my work life and that life. So I don't have to tell *everyone* who I am. Just certain people."

He shifted forward, elbows on his knees. "Thank you for telling me. It's a privilege I don't take lightly." Hesitation warred on his face. "There's something I should tell you. Not so we're even or anything, but you've trusted me, and I want you to know that I trust you, too."

Before he could say more, his phone rang.

He jumped up, startled out of his chair, to answer it.

"Detective Reed." His expression darkened. "Text me the address; I'll be right there."

He hung up.

"You have to get back to work."

He came over and leaned down, one hand on the arm of the chair. "I'll be back later." He touched his lips to hers.

Neither of them pulled back right away.

"Go. I'm going to rest."

"You're not in danger, I don't believe. But I am going to call a friend and see if I can get you coverage. Just in case."

She didn't know what that meant, but she appreciated what he was doing. "Thanks."

And then he was gone.

TWENTY-THREE

Jasper leaned his shoulder against the PD break room vending machine while waiting for it to dispense his cold soda.

He stared at the text he'd sent Destiny on the Wi-Fi messaging app. Three days ago.

No reply.

It indicated she hadn't even read the message.

The machine whirred. He pulled the sweating bottle out and tried not to think about it too much while he made the call to Vanguard.

"Simon Olson."

"It's Jas." This was going to sound way too stalkerish. How did he even explain the need to check on Destiny? He had no right to even ask.

She'd left, and he'd let her.

"Hey, heard your car exploded."

"That was fast." Jasper could talk about work easily enough. "But that's not why I'm calling."

"Your father already called about a protection detail."

"He..." Of course, he had. Jasper couldn't even deal with

that guy—not for a long time. He trailed down the halls of the PD, through the bullpen to his desk. Not the corner office his father thought he should have. Even SWAT hadn't impressed him. Neither had making detective or anything else Jasper had ever done.

He sighed.

Simon chuckled. "Pretty sure Clare told him where he could shove a request for your protection that didn't come from you."

"She did?"

"After the thing two years ago, she's not interested in contracting with your dad. So, what do you need?"

"Right," Jasper said. "If I give you a number, can you track the phone?"

"This have to do with your bomber?"

"You mean, the dead guy or the guy who blew up my car this morning?" Jasper was going to have to get a new beater, or he'd be delivering boxes to low-income communities in the luxury car his dad bought him and wouldn't let him sell.

If there wasn't a dead police officer, he'd be wishing the bomber blew up his other car. The one he hated.

Simon said, "Either?"

"Who knows. Did you guys get the DNA we collected from the house, the one that returned as that dead guy?"

"Yeah, we're running it as well so we can see if Vanguard gets a hit on something you don't have access to."

Jasper said, "The suspect who bombed my car is a ghost. Unless the state police officers interviewing eyewitnesses got someone who can ID the guy, we have next to nothing." And that wasn't even the case he was supposed to be working.

"I'll see what I can find. Send it over."

Jasper figured that meant he'd hack surveillance, traffic, and doorbell cameras. Simon could access practically anything as long as it was connected to the internet. That was why Jasper had called him now. "I'm texting you Destiny Reed's number. Can you tell me where she is and when she last used her phone?"

"She's Blake's sister, right? The one who went to Africa?"

"That's her. I just haven't heard from her in a few days." And if he asked for the mission organization's number, Blake would demand an explanation as to what he was doing.

As long as she was okay, Blake didn't need to know.

But if something had happened, Vanguard should be the first to hear about it. They had international resources that could react fast. And the quicker that could happen, the better, as far as he was concerned.

"Got it. Running." Simon hummed. "Here we go...huh."

"What?" Jasper ignored the cops around him and the pile of work on his desk. He tuned it all out and tried to think of what Destiny would do if it was him that might be in danger.

Which was potentially every shift he worked as a cop.

She would probably pray, but he didn't know how to do that. He could ask Liam, but he hadn't called the sergeant back. Dakota, maybe—but they needed to patch things up between them first. Gage? The lieutenant might just tell him to get back to work. Or invite him to church.

Jasper wasn't ready for a service.

Or the battle it would be with his father if he became a Christian. As if there was nothing worse that he could aspire to be.

"Well, it takes longer than a few seconds. Normally. But that phone is pinging off a tower in Kadoma. It's in Zimbabwe."

"Is that good or bad?" He'd been to a few places in the world, but nowhere he found interesting.

"Hmm. I've got..." His voice trailed off. "And there's..."

Jasper waited about as long as he could stand. "What is it, Simon? Is something going on there? Is she in danger?"

His partner glanced over.

Jasper waved off his concern and turned in his chair. "Simon, talk."

"It's too early to say." Simon paused. "I'll call you back."

The line went dead.

Jasper stared at the phone. At that message that she'd never responded to.

> We can talk about it when you get back.

Was it the last thing he would ever say to her?

"Hollingsworth!" his new lieutenant called out over the bullpen, dragging him from his thoughts. "Staties got a witness who can ID our bomber. I wanna know if you recognize him. And your dad's on his way in."

And the lieutenant was giving him an out to leave so that he wasn't here when the old man showed up. Jasper grabbed his backpack. He'd have to get the motor pool to sign him out an unmarked car.

His partner chuckled. "At some point, we're gonna talk about how you're a grown man running from your daddy."

"Not today."

He laughed louder. Plenty of guys gave Jasper grief about it, but they also covered for him so he didn't have to deal with the senator. Blue blood had proven thicker than what ran in his veins—and came from his dad—every time.

He could face his dad's attempt to "protect" him or get out and catch the guy who did it?

No contest.

TWENTY-FOUR

Blake climbed out of the car just before midnight, exhausted from the day even though he'd taken a nap around dinner time. Who knew how long this meet would go? The house had a run-down feel to it, the kind only an established neighborhood could have. These homes had been here for decades, unlike Violet's, which hadn't been there more than ten years as evidenced by trees that were no taller than the first floor.

At this house, the front walk had a break where two pavers rose to meet each other from being pushed up by the thick root of a tree.

Two men waited on the porch. He might be here, but his mind was on the day.

They'd taken the eyewitness sketch Marco had done before he was let out on bail—and then nearly murdered—and showed the sketch artist's work to the man at the apartment complex. He'd confirmed for them that it was *not* the man he'd seen messing with Jasper's car.

The guy he'd seen was young.

The sketch was of a different person.

Neither of them was the man whose DNA had pinged in the military database.

Now Marco was in surgery, and they were back to having no clue as to the bomber's identity or how he'd taken on a protégé.

Blake had two missed calls from Jasper while he was sleeping, but his return call hadn't been answered. He'd also tried to contact his father—although he'd be better off visiting in person. It wasn't like the guy could pick up the phone whenever and chat. He was in prison and would be for years to come.

The two men on the porch shifted to block his way to the front door.

Blake stopped at the bottom of four cracked concrete steps and waited. They either wanted him here or they didn't. He had to play it cool while making them believe he didn't want the truth of what he'd done to come out.

Which was actually true.

But he didn't have the desperation they wanted to see in him. The same kind that had pushed Violet to break down in the hospital. Torn up by the injuries and suffering of a child and facing down her father's indifference.

His dad might be in prison, but the guy was a better man than Violet's father would ever be.

The two men stared at him.

Blake stayed where he was. Thinking about Violet.

She'd have been a doctor by now. Maybe he'd have met her in the hospital, and they'd have started dating—without any of what was happening now. Then again, he'd probably have been intimidated by her and scared she'd reject a guy from the wrong side of town with a city wage and daily threats to his life.

He'd have pushed Jasper in her direction and walked

away. She had a lot more in common with Jasper, and not just their zip codes.

As it was, he'd stand between her and everything that came at her. He couldn't believe a father would push his child so hard. Dr. Anderson had made her tie herself in knots just to live up to his expectations.

He liked who she was now. He liked her house, which was not a pretentious mansion. Or this run-down flop house. He fit better here than on those wide streets with expansive front gardens and guys who did their lawn care.

The screen door swung out, the hinge creaking. It was either freezing inside or they had the heating cranked to compensate for the fact the front door was open.

He knew the man who sauntered down the steps. Four inches taller than Blake. Less muscle, but the guy had always been wiry. And vicious.

"Kurt." Blake lifted his chin.

"It's Shorty, and you know it."

"Haven't seen you since JV basketball. How would I know?"

"Sure, Mr. Cop. You don't pay attention to nothin' but your drone and your cop buddies."

Blake said, "You sent someone to hurt Lettie at the center."

"Pat gets carried away sometimes. I'll talk to him." Shorty had a hoodie on with the zipper open. No shirt under it. A 9mm pistol tucked in the front of jeans that rode low on his hips. Tan boots.

They really thought hurting her made him want to help them? Or did Pat get *carried away* and take it too far?

He wouldn't ask if they knew anything about a bomb maker. Guys like this were drug dealers. Not terrorists. Killing their customer base meant they couldn't make money selling poison.

Blake settled on asking, "So, where's the meet?"

Shorty grabbed the side of his neck and squeezed. "Don't worry about where. Just worry about keeping me from getting shot and stabbed, yeah?"

Was that supposed to sound like anything other than a threat?

Shorty spun him around, and they headed for a silver older-model Cadillac. Blake ended up in the back while one of the men drove. Shorty was beside him.

The car hummed through city streets.

Blake closed and opened his eyes in the dark interior, waking up his eyes so they didn't get blurry when he needed clarity.

Shorty might be a dealer now, but he'd been a basketball star —all elbows. The kind of player who would foul you after you scored against him. This guy would absolutely make trouble for Blake and tell everyone what happened on that rooftop.

Because he'd been there the day it happened.

It wasn't lost on him that after Violet shared her darkest pain, he should trust her enough to reciprocate. She seemed all in with this...whatever was happening between them. He wasn't ready to call it a relationship, even if he wanted to.

Why was he so scared to tell her? He hadn't even explained about his dad. It wasn't like she'd given him any indication she wasn't trustworthy. He just had so much fear.

Imposter syndrome.

Someone had told him once that imposters didn't get imposter syndrome. Which, by definition, meant he wasn't an imposter. He was the real deal—just a guy with a deep knowledge of who he was and where he'd come from.

A respect for the need to follow the rule of law.

He could never be high and mighty. He had no illusions what kind of person he was when left to his own devices.

Without his faith in the badge he wore, he would be exactly like the men in this car.

The driver pulled into an abandoned industrial complex. Mostly businesses that'd failed and packed up shop, and no one had taken over.

Another car waited behind one of the warehouses. Shorty's driver pulled theirs up to it so the headlights shone into their car. Meanwhile, the other vehicle had fully tinted windows.

"Who is it?"

Shorty grabbed the door handle beside him. "Doesn't matter. You're gonna make sure I don't die."

"Then you slide over and get out my side so I can cover you."

A flash of white teeth in the dark. "Now we're talkin'."

Blake backed out of the door, gun drawn. Shorty slid over. When Blake had scanned around them, he waved the guy out. "You don't trust your boys to do this?"

They stayed in the car, in fact.

"I don't share my business."

So his boys didn't get to hear whatever conversation was about to go down? Interesting. He wanted a third party. One he believed he could coerce into doing what he wanted. Because he thought Blake would do *anything* to keep what happened on the rooftop a secret.

Blake walked slightly behind Shorty. The driver's door of the black car opened, and an older, pudgy Caucasian man got out.

"Who's this?" Blake asked.

Shorty bristled. "Good question." He raised his voice to say, "I know you?"

The man approaching had a cheap suit and scuffed shoes. His thinning brown hair was all rumpled. He lifted both hands. "I am Elyan."

Blake knew that name. What case?

He needed his work computer and thirty seconds and he'd be able to figure out why this guy seemed familiar. His accent was Eastern European or Russian. It might tie to the last case he worked with Liam.

"What do you want from us?" Shorty shifted, about ready to shoot this guy and leave instead of waiting around for an explanation.

Elyan sucked in a sharp breath, desperation in every movement. "I need protection. I need help. He's crazy, and he won't stop."

"But you still work for him," Shorty said. "So why is it my problem?"

"Because he's got a bomb maker working for him, and he'll kill all of us."

TWENTY-FIVE

It felt good to be back in the center, even if Violet had to fight the worry wanting to eclipse everything. Granny had dropped her off. Most of the kids would be at school, but the repairs should be underway.

The construction guys in the common room glanced over when she arrived.

She stayed by the door, still not completely comfortable being out of the house. But she lifted one hand and waved.

Her body didn't hurt quite as much as it had, but she was still stiff.

After being attacked and very nearly being blown up the other day, she was on edge. Her nerves were practically fried. Not a good thing when she had to be stuck at home because she couldn't take a paramedic shift until a doctor signed off on her physical capability.

"Violet, you're here."

She spun to find Merry coming down the hall, holding a tablet to her front. The center's manager smiled, but Violet didn't quite believe it.

"I'm here." She smiled back, hopefully more convincing.

"I just stopped in to see how things were going and see if I can help out with anything."

Guilt was an ugly feeling. She tried to push it away.

Why couldn't she do like she did with AA and make amends? Austin had caused this damage because he considered her responsible for Marco being arrested. Now Marco was fighting for his life in surgery. Was Austin there, waiting to hear word about his brother's condition?

"You have a lot going on right now." Merry's expression shifted.

"Not as much as you'd think. I was a bit stir crazy at home."

Merry nodded. "Understandable, only…is this the best place for you?"

She couldn't go anywhere else.

"I'm sure with bombs exploding around you and the safety of kids here a factor that you can understand this might not be the best choice," Merry said. "You could be putting other people at risk."

"I don't think I'm the target." She just seemed to be in the vicinity of things that were happening. "Except for the attack that happened here."

"Probably best not to be reminded of it by coming here. Maybe when things have settled down, you can come back, and we can talk over your role here and what that looks like going forward."

Violet blinked. "You're firing me?"

"You're a volunteer, Violet. And I appreciate everything you've done for the center over the years."

"Since before you came on as the manager. That's how long I've been here."

Merry lifted her chin. "If you want to petition the board to replace me, you're welcome to do so."

Violet flinched. "I'm not trying to take your job. I'm a paramedic, Merry. That's what I do. This is about helping people." She waved a hand. "Giving back to the community and providing a safe place for kids."

"I've read the flyer."

"I wrote the flyer." Violet spun around and strode to the front doors. She stepped outside into the January chill and stared at the traffic buzzing past on the street in front of her.

She had no car, no ride. Granny had dropped her off and wouldn't be back to pick her up until after her Bible study ended.

No reason to stress over it too much. She just pulled out her phone and dialed Blake's number.

"Detective Reed."

"It's Violet." She paused, hesitant to sound pathetic. He was working. She shouldn't be bothering him.

"Everything okay?"

She swallowed against the lump in her throat. "I'm a liability."

"Where are you?"

Tears gathered in her eyes. "At the center. I can't be here because I'm a walking disaster right now." And the last thing she'd wanted to do was cry on his shoulder—through the phone. That would be far too pathetic. "Don't worry about it."

She could just go across the street to the coffee shop and wait for Granny to be done with her study.

"Vi—"

"I don't want to keep you." Violet hung up and crossed the street.

No one died in a fiery explosion. She got coffee, and no one attacked her. Things were good. She had her purse, and she had a drink to ward off the cold. It was sweet, probably sweeter than her hips required, but that choice was between her and Jesus.

She found a quiet corner and pulled the journal out of her purse, just a small notebook really, but she used it frequently to process her thoughts. The thing had gotten a lot of use since Blake showed up.

Why do I feel so useless?

She was accustomed to being in charge and taking control of a situation in her work as a paramedic or with teens. In this situation, Blake had to solve his case, and other cops would find the bomber.

She didn't want to become a cop.

That required two exclamation marks and an underline in the journal, because this wasn't about her needing a career change. More likely, it was about being frustrated because she'd been doing the same thing for years.

"Are you okay?"

She jerked and looked up from her journal to find Blake standing over her, badge on his belt. And causing quite a stir in the coffee shop. "You came?"

He leaned down and kissed her cheek, then slid into the seat across from her. Several women in the coffee shop seemed disappointed. "You sounded upset."

So he'd dropped everything and come to find her?

"I'm a liability. Merry doesn't want me at the center until this is over."

He frowned. "None of it is on you. It's not like you're drawing criminals to the center. In fact, your presence there probably keeps some of the activity that would be happening at bay."

That might not be the case, but it was nice to think about. "I hope that is true."

"Do you know the two guys that were playing basketball during the tribunal? Hound and Pat?"

"Sure, I guess I've seen them around."

"Pat is the one who attacked you, so you need to call 911 right away if you see him. Okay?" He laid his hand over hers.

Violet set her pen down and turned her hand into his. His reassuring grip gave her strength. Holding hands was seriously underrated. "Thanks for coming."

"I actually…" He took a breath. "I had something I wanted to tell you about."

"What is it?"

"If this… I need to tell you so you're not blindsided later because I didn't."

She stayed quiet while he figured out what to say. It seemed to be difficult for him to find the words.

He cleared his throat. "Maybe just saying it plainly is better."

She nodded.

"My father is in prison."

She blinked. "That's not what I thought you were going to say."

"He came back from the first Gulf War pretty disillusioned about the government lying to people. So, he took it upon himself to learn how to build a bomb, and he set it to explode in a tanker at the docks on the coast."

She kept herself still so he wouldn't think this had any reflection on how she felt about him.

"I guess it went off early. There were casualties, people he said weren't supposed to be there. He was found floating in the water, injured. After he was arrested, he took responsibility and pled guilty to the whole plot."

Violet wasn't sure what to say.

"My dad might be nothing like yours, but that doesn't

mean I have a good heritage. Or some kind of legacy of success to draw from."

She said, "As far as I can see, success isn't all that great. It costs too much, and the trade-off is never worth it. I'd rather focus on helping people."

Was that the problem? She was so bruised and battered that she couldn't help. *God, help me find contentment.*

Maybe Blake was the person she was supposed to help right now.

"We don't get to choose who we come from," she said. "But we can choose who we are. That's what I tell the kids at the center, and I have to remind myself of that often when I feel like I'm not good enough. That I should have the big house, the flashy car, and the corner office. That I should be a doctor, not just a paramedic."

"Seems to me that who you are is pretty great."

She squeezed his hand. "So are you."

"My dad is pretty great, actually." He smiled. "He became a Christian at a prison Bible study, and now he teaches it. He writes to the girls all the time, sending letters and cards so they can get to know him. When he calls me, he always says he's praying for me."

"That's amazing." Between her father and his, it seemed pretty clear who was the success story.

"I'm not sure it's working, though. Things seem...hard."

"That's how you know it's worth it. If it takes work to get the result." She shrugged one shoulder. "And even if we don't achieve whatever it is, like closing a case or keeping a patient alive, we still know we tried. We didn't give up."

TWENTY-SIX

"What about when nothing makes sense, but you really need a lead on a case?" Blake quipped. "What do you say then?"

The weight off his shoulders felt great. He didn't have to worry about Violet's reaction to him having a criminal for a father—just the rest of his own story.

Some of the cops he worked with remembered the incident, enough to look sideways at him on occasion. A training officer in the academy had informed Blake that his brother was in the tanker working the night shift when it blew.

So much for getting a fair shake on test scores.

Blake hadn't said anything. He'd just doubled down on proving himself. A couple of weeks later, the guy had retired. Blake had no idea who figured it out or which of his training buddies might've said something.

Violet said, "Is it something you can talk about? Maybe I can help brainstorm."

"Sorry, but you're a witness and a victim, plus it's an ongoing investigation."

"I understand."

"Maybe you could do something for me today." He said it before the thought had even fully formed. Now that he considered it, the idea was a good one. "I can't go because I'm at work."

He explained about the last time his father had called and how he'd seemed reticent to share.

"Visiting hours today are from two to four this afternoon. And you don't look like a cop, so it won't seem like he's getting a visit from the police."

He couldn't send anyone else.

"If you drop me at home and maybe check my car to make sure it won't explode, I could."

"You could use my truck." If she was really worried about the bomber he could give her at least that much peace of mind. "I'll check out anything you want me to. Just so you aren't scared of what might happen."

He doubted the bomber would target her specifically, but it also wasn't worth assuming and risking her life in the process.

"I'll drive you to the PD. You can take my truck." But he would also call someone with the bomb squad to confirm the vehicle was clear.

He studied her face to see if she looked nervous and saw no sign of worry. She seemed to have perked up.

"I'd love to meet your father." Violet smiled. "And I desperately need something to do."

He smiled, too. She was adorable.

Thirty minutes later, they were in the PD parking lot, and the bomb squad guy was finishing up. The officer had been on shift and in the office. Explosives had been part of his training in the military—and now with the Benson PD. The rest of the bomb squad was a mix of firefighters and cops.

Violet hung up with her granny. "Okay, she's going to head home. I'm good to go."

Compared to her relationship with her father, she might love his dad. "It's hard to get to know him well. He's all about his faith, and it's not like we can do stuff together."

"I'm going to ask him what they need in the prison and talk to my church. See if we can help them out with prayer or anything else. They might need books!"

Blake tugged her to his side and kissed her open mouth.

Violet slid her arms around his waist and held on.

He was a bit in awe of the way she jumped on board with his dad, excited to better the life of someone she'd never met. But then, she did that with everything. The kiss went on long enough that someone whistled, and he remembered he was at work.

Blake pulled back, clearing his throat, and felt the heat on his face. "Thanks, babe."

She grinned. "You should get back to work."

"Vehicle is all clear."

Blake reluctantly let her go and shook the officer's hand. "I appreciate it." He turned back to Violet in time for her to grab his shoulders and plant another kiss on his lips.

"I'll call you," she said.

"Text me every step. Before and after. I want to know when you get there, when you leave, and especially if you get an odd feeling."

She grinned and climbed into his truck, waving as she pulled out of the PD parking lot. She paused at the exit before pulling onto the road. Long enough that he started to walk toward her.

Then his phone buzzed.

Her text read:

Leaving now.

He sent back a Bitmoji his sisters used often and got a laughing face emoji in return.

Back upstairs in Intelligence, he got a weird look from Wilks, who had his mouth around the end of a burrito. He didn't swallow before he said, "What's up with you?"

"Nothing." Blake sank into his chair, determined not to let anything dampen his mood. He should have had Violet share her GPS location, just in case. If she stopped, he'd ask her to share it. "What have you got?"

Wilks thankfully swallowed. "Officers on surveillance detail report he hasn't left the motel since last night."

"Any idea who this guy is?" He and Shorty had talked Elyan off the ledge, but since he hadn't told them who he worked for, it was hard to muster up concern. At least not enough for Blake to blow his cover.

But it was enough to run the car's license plate and put a BOLO out. Night shift officers hadn't taken long to find him and follow him back to the motel, where their relief team had been watching him since.

"Ran the name he gave you." Wilks held up a photo. "This the guy?"

"Yeah, who is he?"

"An accountant for the Russians. No one's seen him in months, and he shows up now scared over some guy he works for?" Wilks shook his head. "I don't buy it."

"We need a break in this case." Blake tapped his pen on the edge of his desk.

"He was probably gonna kill your buddy, or your buddy is the killer and Elyan was the next target."

And Blake's intervention had kept someone from dying, was that it? Probably more like Wilks believed Blake going undercover had kept the killer from slipping up and leaving evidence or a witness at another murder.

Which meant he was counting on another death.

After an officer had died so recently, there was nothing Blake wouldn't do to stop another fatality. "I don't think it was either of them that killed the others." But he couldn't prove it.

"DNA came back on Marco. Couple unknowns and a familial match."

"He has a teenage brother who frequents the center. Austin, I think his name is."

Wilks nodded slowly. "You should run him, see if anything pops. Kids at the center probably all have juvie records." He paused for a split second. "You got one?"

"Because you looked me up and found nothing?"

"Juvie records are sealed once you turn eighteen. No one would know."

Blake said, "I did the same with you. You know what I found? Your brother got away with a slap on the wrist."

"While your daddy got life." Wilks argued. "My brother was innocent."

The victim who'd made the accusation likely wouldn't corroborate that. But the whole thing happened more than twenty years ago. Back when Wilks had been a beat cop.

His phone beeped. He glanced at the screen and saw a link from Violet—a GPS location share.

Wilks said, "Agree to disagree, I guess. Since you have nothing to say."

Blake lifted his head. "If you've got a problem with me, come out and say it. Nothin' I haven't heard before."

Wilks snorted.

"Why don't you just tell me if this Russian accountant has any known associates?"

That jerked the guy back to focus. Or perhaps it was the sergeant walking up behind Blake.

Deerdan said, "Update, please."

When Wilks didn't start first, Blake said, "The artist sketch of the guy given by Marco isn't the same guy that planted the bomb in Detective Hollingsworth's car. We have more than one bomber, or an apprentice."

And wasn't that a terrifying thought?

Deerdan nodded. "Marco Phelps should wake up soon."

"And the brother, Austin Phelps, the one who tore up the center?"

Deerdan said, "Due to be arraigned in the morning. You think he'll be after revenge for what happened to his brother if he's let out?"

"Hopefully not." Austin wasn't the younger apprentice since he'd been in jail for destruction of property. So, who was the person that had wired up Jasper's car?

Deerdan said, "Go talk to Marco."

TWENTY-SEVEN

Violet stared at the prison visitor's entrance for a second. A stooped woman, probably in her forties, walked beside a teenage boy toward the door. Neither looked at her. Did she know how to do this?

After jumping at the chance to help out, now that she was here, she wasn't sure what she was doing by meeting her boyfriend's father for the first time on visitor's day.

Was Blake her boyfriend?

It seemed like it, even though they hadn't defined what was happening between them. But saying "boyfriend" felt way too junior high. What did adults do when they dated? She was so out of practice. For years she'd just worried about surviving. Getting through the worst day of her life and moving on—figuring out how to hold her head up when people knew she'd lost it and attacked her father.

Crashed and burned.

Landed in rehab.

And such were some of you. The quote from a Bible passage that had always stuck out to her moved through her mind now. She was no better or worse than anyone else. She had struggles just like believers inside and out of this prison in front of her. Men like Blake's father, who had been given a life sentence. The best person and the worst person in the world.

Before God, everyone was a sinner.

Violet pulled open the door and stepped into a waiting area. She did the sign-in thing, asking for time with Jamal Reed—something Vanguard had gotten approved for her. She was more nervous than she wanted to admit about seeing Blake's father.

She sank onto a hard chair in the corner and sat without pulling out her phone. With her addictive personality, she'd taught herself not to do things without thinking first. It didn't always help to go to her phone and get lost in the dopamine rush, but sometimes, it was exactly the thing she needed.

A cute dog video, one funny meme, and one verse from Psalms explained by a charismatic person of faith.

An older gentleman settled beside her. "Afternoon."

She nodded. "How are you?"

"I don't really know if it's kosher to talk to other people in the waiting area. I'm new to all this."

"Me, too." She smiled. "It's my first time."

He gave her an endearing smile. "Am I supposed to ask you who you're seeing, or is that taboo?"

She looked around. "No one else is talking, but maybe we should stick together while waiting."

The correctional officer behind the desk shot her an odd look. The plexiglass between her and him didn't provide either of them much protection, but it did provide a barrier, even if it was only mental.

The older man had on jeans and a heavy jacket. She tucked her own closer around her since the chill in here was real. Did the prisoners get all the heat, or was the whole place this cold? Maybe they could use blankets as well as Bibles, journals, and other books. Did the prison consider a pen a lethal weapon? She needed to find out what the rules were—more than just what the check-in sergeant had listed to her for when she went inside and left everything but her jacket in a cubby.

The man had a canvas hat on and winked at her from under the brim. Still, there was something about him that held her back. Something that told her this was no harmless old man. Whatever life he'd lived, he'd seen some things.

Not totally to the level of the worst experiences the center kids went through. But not all sunshine and kittens either.

"I'm actually here to meet my boyfriend's father." She smiled. "He couldn't be here, so he asked me to come. Since I wasn't working today, I said yes." Her face flamed. "Should I have said yes?"

The old man chuckled. "Whoa, girlie. Too many feelings in one go. Hold your horses."

"Sorry." She needed an outlet, like work—like the center. Otherwise, she had to work hard to process so many things. Her life was so different now than it had been. She worked every day to make it good but putting too much pressure on would result in a minicollision that mirrored the larger train-wreck all too closely.

He shifted in his chair. Her attention snagged on an odd patch of clear skin on his cheek where there should be stubble like on the rest of his chin. A scar? "Not to worry. Big day for you."

"I'm just glad I was off."

"You look like maybe you should be at home resting." He scanned her face. "Your boyfriend do that to you?"

Apparently, she hadn't done as good of a job as she'd thought covering the abrasions and bruises. "Absolutely not."

"Good. He sort it for you?"

She frowned. "What do you mean?"

"Did he find the guy who did it and beat the tar out of him?"

"Oh." She'd gotten the impression he might if he saw him. "He's a police officer. I don't think they're really supposed to do that."

They were definitely not supposed to do that, but the older man chuckled. "Guess not."

She smiled. "But I think he might *want* to."

"I bet he does."

"Anyway, I—"

"Violet Anderson!"

She gasped, choking on the word. "That's me." She shot the old man a grin. "Nice talking to you."

She was led through the rigamarole of check in, security questions, scans, a pat down, and more questions. All of it blurred into everything else until she forced herself to snap out of it.

She needed to be focused.

Especially considering one of the guards led her into an expansive room littered with tiny round tables, like little picnic benches with plastic bench seats. Like a cheap fast-food place.

A handsome older black man sat at one table, pretty close to the center of the room.

When they headed for him, Jamal Reed stood up. Blinked. Realized she was here to see him.

The guard paused for a second, then disappeared.

"Jamal, I'm Violet Anderson."

His dark brown eyes warmed. "Blake?"

She bit her lip. Nodded.

He tipped his head back and chuckled. "My son. He has good taste." Jamal held out his hands, and she placed hers in them. "Violet Anderson, it is exceedingly nice to meet you."

Violet warmed from head to toe, welcomed in a way she'd never been before.

"God is good to me. I'm very blessed."

She felt that, too. How could she not? She'd been nervous, and Jamal had put her at ease immediately.

As soon as he released her hands, he touched his hands together and touched his heart. "Thank You, Jesus. *My son.*"

They settled onto the seats, and she hardly realized they were hard and plastic. "You've been worried about him?"

"He refuses to see the truth. He needs to find his way to surrender, the way we all do."

"Unfortunately, that meant I had to crash and burn." Hopefully he wouldn't ask her to tell the story.

"So did I, dear." He smiled, warm and friendly. The jumpsuit took nothing away from his presence. Though he did seem a little worn at the edges, this man had found hope in a dark place.

The same way she had.

"By making a bomb?" He had killed.

"The truth and what people believe are sometimes quite different."

What did that mean? Violet didn't know this man well enough to ask. She said, "Blake asked me to come and check on you. Something about a phone call?"

"I did have something I wanted to tell him."

"I'm sorry. If it's for him only, I can say it's important that he comes." Just in case he might want to keep it private.

Jamal seemed to hesitate, maybe deciding what to say—or how to say it.

Noise erupted beside her.

A man attacked another man, both wearing jumpsuits.

Someone female screamed. One of the men threw the other man toward her and Jamal. Rubber bullets flew through the air.

The guy landed on the table between them, and she stumbled back. Her legs caught on the bench chair.

She fell, crying out.

Jamal rounded the table.

She scrambled to her feet. The inmate attacker grabbed her, spinning her in front of him so she couldn't do anything. She couldn't even breathe.

"Let her go, Shears." The guard's tone didn't invite any room to argue, just comply.

Violet gasped.

Jamal stepped in front of them. "Let her go."

"I don't think so." The inmate holding her chuckled.

The one from the table, who'd been stunned, jumped up and grabbed Jamal, shoving something at his abdomen. Jamal cried out. The inmate drew his hand back, blood on a weapon gripped in his fingers.

Jamal fell to the floor.

Violet screamed. She lifted her foot and slammed it down on the inmate's shin. The guy holding her grunted and let go. Guards slammed into him behind her.

She dove for Jamal, both hands on his abdomen. "Call an ambulance!"

TWENTY-EIGHT

arco's features twisted with pain.

"Sorry, but I have to ask." Blake leaned forward in the chair beside Marco's hospital bed. This guy knew the bomber and had identified him, but after he was released from jail, he'd been targeted by a killer. "We're trying to find this guy. If we don't, more people will die."

"Yeah, guys like me that you only pretend to care about to make your case." Marco gasped.

Blake held himself still, even though habit made him want to look at his watch—or his phone. Worry about Violet consumed him, but checking for a message was pointless because she wouldn't be able to take her phone, or anything else, into the prison to see his father.

What would she think of him after this?

"Guys like you aren't that different from guys like me." Blake had seen it with Violet and her father, and his own. "It's just choices. We all have to decide, and we get to choose for ourselves."

"You think I'm gonna see the light."

Turn his life around? That could absolutely happen. "My father got a life sentence, but he turned his life around. He won't be released for decades yet. But he does good where he can—right where he's at."

Marco snorted.

"Someone tried to kill you. That's got to at least make you angry enough to tell me who it was. Nothin' you can do about it until you're out of the hospital." Blake shrugged. "Why not give me a shot at the legwork of finding him?"

He let Marco think about that while he sat for a minute or so, listening to hospital staff pass by the door. Visitors. A phone ringing somewhere down the hall. It was a wonder anyone could recover in a hospital; it was so noisy.

"You did a deal before, gave us that sketch for a break from the district attorney." Blake hadn't been able to ID the guy, or find him, but that didn't mean it wasn't a solid lead. He could only label it deception if he could prove that. Until then it was presumed to be good intel.

"You think I want everyone knowing some punk kid stuck me."

Blake studied the man in the hospital bed. "But he didn't kill you. So let me get him."

"Where's Austin?"

Interesting segue. "Tell me what happened, and I'll update you."

Marco studied him right back. "What do you mean update? He isn't out there in the hall waiting for you to be done?"

Blake shook his head. "Tell me what happened."

Marco made a face.

Yeah, Blake didn't like this either.

Marco said, "He popped me, then when I was down, he stabbed me." Marco lifted a hand, a blood oxygen reader on his index finger. Two of his fingernails were broken. "Tried to grab him, but he stuck me like he enjoyed it." His voice mumbled into vulgar insults. "I'll kill him."

"How about I arrest him instead? Then you and anyone who might be next won't go to jail for the sake of revenge on this punk." A lot of criminals didn't care about the consequences of their actions or what the punishment might be.

Kind of like the way so many people did whatever they wanted and called it freedom. Consideration for others wasn't super fashionable these days. People would rather be selfish and not care who was hurt in the process.

He'd stuck with his brothers in SWAT until that disbanded. Now he had others in his life outside the PD and besides his sisters.

He wanted to improve Violet's and Doris's lives if he could. Along with wanting a whole lot more with Violet. Maybe even everything a man could want from a wife. She'd seemed receptive, and they were getting closer.

Did she want it all the way he did?

Marco finally said, "I don't know who the kid was."

Maybe he thought Austin did. "Your brother tore up the center. He should be arraigned soon, and I'll tell him you want to talk. Make sure he gets here to see you."

Blake's phone started to buzz in his pocket.

Marco nodded.

He stood. "Thanks for your time."

In the hall, he saw the number calling was labeled as the prison switchboard. "Detective Reed."

"It's Violet." She gasped, sounding upset. Like when she'd called him earlier from the street outside the center, and he'd found her in the coffee shop. But also much more than that.

"What's going on?" He double-timed it to the stairs and headed down while she recounted visiting his father.

What should've been a good conversation with a positive outcome had turned into an attack.

His gut twisted. "You're okay?"

"They took him in an ambulance." Worry laced her tone. "I'm in the warden's office. He let me in here to clean up, but I wanted to tell you."

"I'll come there." She didn't need to drive back. "I'll pick you up." And while he was there, he could see the surveillance tapes and look at what'd happened.

"They're taking your dad to the hospital."

Which was right where he was, but it wasn't where *she* was. "He'll be in surgery. It'll take time before we can see him."

"We?"

"I'm coming to get you," Blake said. "Clean up and I'll be there soon. Okay?"

"Okay." Relief flooded her tone. "Thanks, Blake."

"My pleasure, honey."

He called Jasper from the department-issued sedan he'd checked out, but his friend didn't answer. The same with Liam—no response there either. So he called Doris and checked in to ensure she was all right.

In the end, she kept him talking all the way there, and he hung up with her right as he pulled into the parking lot. It was odd to miss something he'd never had. He'd never known his grandparents or the girls' grandparents through their mom.

Would Doris want to be that for all of them, not just Violet? It seemed like the older woman might have enough energy to go around. And when she started to slow down— because it didn't seem to have happened yet—she would have even more people to take care of her.

Blake met the warden just inside the door. He flashed his badge, got all checked in, and the guy led him down to the office where Violet had said she was. Before they got to the door, he said, "Any idea what motivated the attack?"

The warden, a silver-haired man in his sixties who looked like he might've been a marine in his younger years, stopped outside the door. "The usual? I'm pulling footage. Two of my guys are interrogating the assailant, asking all the questions."

Blake nodded.

"We've got him locked down, though. And your girl was startled, but she has no injuries."

He had to fight down the reaction to hearing that Violet might've been hurt as well.

"I'd like to see the surveillance." Who in here would be his father's enemy? "You think it was a targeted attack, or was he just closest?"

"That's what I hope to find out." The guy nodded and opened the door, leaving it wide so Blake could go in. "I'll be in the control room."

"Thanks." He stepped inside.

Violet waited until the guy had disappeared. Then she rushed over and slammed into him, winding her arms around his middle.

"You didn't get hurt?" Blake tried not to let a tone seep in, but she hadn't told him she had been involved other than as an observer.

"One of them grabbed me. Another guy stabbed your father." She sniffed.

He hugged her, and when she pulled back, he asked, "Are you okay?"

The relief on her face felt better than anything. She even smiled a little. "I've been praying for your dad. Are you sure you want to drive back when you just got here? And what do we do with the other car?"

"I'll have someone drive the department car for me." It

was just a technicality, but she cared about the details rather than ignoring what wasn't relevant to her immediate sphere. "How was he?"

To his soul, he didn't want to lose his dad. The frustration was enough that he would like to pick up the chair he was sitting in and throw it across the room—like what Austin did at the center. Only, how would that help anything? He was who he was because he'd curbed those tendencies and taught himself control.

They sat in the two chairs in front of the warden's desk, facing each other. "It was deep." She winced. "I've been praying for him since the ambulance picked him up."

"Can we..." He didn't even know how to ask, but the truth was that everyone in his life believed in God. If it helped them, then maybe it could help him make sense of the mess.

She touched his hand. "What is it?"

Blake said, "Can you show me how to pray so I can as well?"

Okay, well, Violet was totally in love with him now. And it happened through a very basic prayer, because she'd never felt the need to have pretense when God knew her heart and mind—and all her failures. A brief kiss afterward. Holding hands down the hall. She wanted to melt into a puddle on the floor at his feet.

He squeezed her hand, and she let go. Back to work.

She didn't need to degrade his professionalism because her life was spinning out of control. She'd been so excited to come here. A short time later, she'd felt Jamal's blood between her fingertips.

"Keep fighting, don't give up. Don't let go. Jesus, Lord, don't take him." Blake needed his father. His sisters, too, even if Jamal was only their brother's father. "Hang on, Jamal."

He stared up at her from the floor. "Blake."

She needed to tell Blake. "Hang on. He needs you."

"Tell...Blake." He coughed, and blood wet his lips.

"Don't try to talk." She glanced around to where the guards had every inmate against the wall. One on the floor, a knee in

his back. The attacker. The one who'd held her sneered from the lineup. "I need an ambulance!"

Surely, there was a doctor in this place.

"Get me a medical kit!"

No one was listening; there was too much noise. Visitors were ushered out. Guards yelling. Inmates chattering.

"Someone, get help!"

One of the guards glanced over his shoulder. "The doc is on his way."

True to his word, an inner door swung open seconds later, and a man in a lab coat raced in carrying a duffel.

Blake touched her shoulder. "You okay?"

She blinked but could still see his father's face in her mind. She could still feel Jamal's chest rise and fall with each breath as he struggled for life. "I'm just praying for your dad."

Someone snorted.

The correctional officer who'd been there.

She glanced at him. Angry words tasted rich on her tongue, so she swallowed them back. If her experiences had taught her anything, it was that flying off the handle and losing her cool weren't things she wanted to do again. It wouldn't be about this guard or his opinion—or the inhumanity of the prison system—instead, it would only be about all the ways she'd failed.

An older man in a suit stepped into the hallway. "Faucher, get back to work. We'll be talking about your actions later."

The guard spun and walked away.

The warden, said, "That talk will likely be in front of the review board."

Violet didn't need to say anything, since this wasn't her purview, so she just nodded.

Blake asked, "Do you have the footage?"

The man led them into a room with a wall of computer screens, all displaying areas of the prison. Seemed like a lot of it was locked down now. Maybe a result of what had happened.

One of the guards, seated at a desk, clicked the spacebar on his keyboard, and the footage played. The inside of the visiting room where it had all gone down but before the fight.

Blake shifted. Looking at his father or the other inmates on the screen. "He met with someone before the fight?"

The warden said, "He signed in on the visitor's log as Malik Henderson."

Violet saw herself. "That's where I came in. The inmate is alone then." She was meeting Jamal on one side of the screen, and at the neighboring table, another man came over and sat down in front of the attacker. "That's the man I talked to in the waiting room."

The scene played out on-screen.

She looked away from her and Jamal, not wanting to see herself get attacked when she'd experienced it firsthand. The waiting room man said only a few words to the inmate before getting up and leaving.

He'd come all that way for such a scant conversation. That didn't make any sense.

And seconds after he stood up, the inmate jumped for his neighbor. The two tangled, she got caught by one and the other stabbed Blake's father.

Blake stiffened again.

"You don't need to be the one to watch it." But she hadn't said that before, and it was too late now.

If only she could hold his hand, but the prison staff would see. Maybe he didn't want to seem like the detective who needed his girlfriend to hold his hand. So, she kept her hands by her sides and prayed silently that Blake had the strength he needed.

That his curiosity about faith would grow to belief.

Lord, help our unbelief.

Blake tugged her back from the warden and the guard and pulled out his phone. "You talked to that man?"

Violet nodded. "For a few minutes, but nothing more than small talk. I don't know his name."

He thumbed the screen and showed her. "Is this him?"

The image on the screen was a pencil drawing. A witness sketch. "Yes, that's him. Who is he?"

"The bomber." Blake turned to the warden. "Evacuate the prison and call the bomb squad. I'll call my sergeant and loop her in."

The warden snatched up a phone from the desktop. "Possible bomb threat. Yes, evacuation protocol. Now." He slammed the phone down. "Sound the alarm."

"Yes, sir." The guard hit a button.

The warden spoke to her and Blake. "Evacuation is going to get busy, so the two of you should get out ahead of the crowd. Just to be safe."

Blake took her hand. "I need a copy of that footage."

"You got it, Detective."

He tugged on her hand, and they fast-walked down the hall. A younger woman and two men in office attire scurried out of a side room, rushing for the exit at the end. They punched the bar, and light spilled into the hall from outside.

Blake tugged her along with him onto the concrete sidewalk and down the curb toward the parking lot.

"I'm sure there's an assembly spot for situations like this." She glanced to the right, through the wire fence where a guard shack towered over the yard. "Like that."

The guards had the inmates all lined up along the fence.

"I could use a conversation of my own with the guy who stabbed my father."

She turned to see his face so she might be able to gauge his intention.

"So I can ask what that guy said to him."

She shuddered. "I can't believe I was talking to the bomber. He seemed so normal. Friendly, even. It sounded like he'd never been a visitor at the prison either." She hadn't had any vibes that he was a cop killer, of all things.

Blake squeezed the spot where her neck met her shoulder. "I want to kiss you, but I don't want to give all these people a show."

She smiled. "Rain check?"

"For sure."

Cars streamed from the parking lot, escaping the potential of another bomb. She wanted to run as well. But if that meant leaving Blake to face this alone, she didn't want to do it. She'd relied on him so much in the past few days and even cried on his shoulder.

He'd saved her life. He'd shown up.

Right now, she wanted to be here for him so he didn't have to worry about his father alone. "I'm still praying for your dad. The EMTs who took him to the hospital said they would call and tell me if they hear anything, and they would also ask the hospital staff to do the same."

Not exactly standard procedure, but they knew her. She'd explained that a Benson PD detective was the next of kin. Everyone in town pulled out all the stops for a first responder.

If he needed peace of mind, they would do their best to give it to him.

Lord, You have Jamal in Your hands. Heal him.

Whatever happened, God would still be good. Would

Blake be able to believe that if he never got to see his father as a free man?

A car sped *into* the lot while every other car queued for the exit.

The driver pulled over to one side and climbed out.

"Captain Espinoza." Blake lifted a hand.

Julio, the firefighter she'd met, jogged over. "I'm off duty, but the bomb squad works on call. There's a device here?"

"The bomber was here," Blake said, "so we don't know if he left anything behind when he—"

A concussive force cracked from her left, bringing her attention around. Violet spun to see Blake's truck launch up and flip over.

Fire whooshed up into the air.

The blast rattled the building. Windows shattered. They all ducked, and a second later, Blake's arms encircled her head, keeping her from being showered with glass.

"Whoa." Espinoza crouched close to them. "That was—"

Another explosion ripped through the front of the building.

Violet felt herself fly through the air...

And then everything went black.

THIRTY

Blake gripped the steering wheel, the flashing red light on the dash giving him credence to follow the convoy of two ambulances. A helicopter had already flown overhead.

The first ambulance pulled into the hospital parking lot, where the emergency department entryway was crowded with medical personnel alerted to the situation.

"We're here." He looked in the rearview but couldn't see Violet. "You good?"

She gasped. "He's hanging by a thread."

Blake pulled up in the row of vehicles. His spot was exposed to the night sky, whereas the ambulances fit under the overhang to keep patients safe from the elements. Thankfully, it wasn't raining—or snowing for that matter. It was supposed to have snowed today.

Is that Your doing?

He'd started praying with Violet. Why stop now? He'd needed someone to talk to after he found her lying unconscious a couple of feet away.

Captain Espinoza had stayed to coordinate the rescue effort.

As soon as she woke up, Violet had brushed off the injury and jumped into action triaging people so the medical personnel who arrived found them already assessed and organized according to the severity of their injuries.

Was she flagging now that the adrenaline had worn off?

Blake climbed out. A nurse had already opened the rear door.

Violet climbed out and said, "Male, forties. History of asthma, which he told me about before he passed out. He's struggling."

She listed to the side, and Blake caught her, tempted to sweep her up into his arms. But then she gripped his arm harder than expected and said to the nurse, "Possible concussion. Possible broken ankle. Some bruising on his hands. But he wasn't pinned by the blast debris."

Espinoza had been digging people out of the rubble, and Blake and Violet were carrying those people to a safe spot where they could wait for the ambulances.

The whole thing had been chaos.

Not one explosion, but two.

His mind still hadn't worked out what that was about.

Another medical person pushed a gurney out to them. They all helped to lift the man onto it, and then Blake lifted Violet into his arms.

She sucked in a breath. "I can walk."

"But you don't have to." He wanted to carry her. After everything she'd done, ignoring her injuries to help others, he needed to help her. She needed to be checked out.

The emergency doors swept open.

He carried her inside, into an ocean of chaos, but quickly spotted Doris standing with Captain McCauley.

Violet said, "Hey, Dennis is here."

The two of them headed over to meet him, and Blake muttered, "I still can't believe you call him Dennis."

The captain was a good cop. Which played in his favor when he reached out and patted her hand, even if Blake did want to get territorial right now. No one needed that.

Captain McCauley said, "Violet."

"Dennis."

Doris asked, "Did you hit your head again?"

Violet sighed.

Blake needed to put her down. Thankfully, one of the nurses waved him over. "This way."

He followed. "Let's get you checked out."

"You should go and see how your dad is. If he's doing okay, he'll want to talk to you."

She was right. He should probably get a report on his father's condition. It would be odd to see him here, not behind prison bars. Not that he was a free man in a hospital. He would have guards. He'd be in handcuffs.

Blake had never pretended his father wasn't a convicted criminal, but he didn't publicize it either. Now everyone would find out. The whole idea of it made him want to walk out like she had when her father was on his way. Scurry out the door—but it would be more like running. And he might just keep going.

He laid Violet on the hospital bed.

She touched his arm. "You should talk to him."

Blake kissed her forehead. "Doris, you good here?"

"Yes, honey." Doris moved to the opposite side of the bed.

The nurse exchanged places with Blake, who strode out into the hall. He moved until she was out of sight, then lifted both hands and laced them behind his head with his elbows out. Breathing in and out.

McCauley stood by the wall, leaning and watching.

Giving Blake a minute.

"You wanna stay, you wanna go see your dad. You keep it all separate, and it doesn't intersect, except now it's all crashing down."

Was that what he did? "My life intersects."

"Does it?" McCauley asked. "Your dad was in prison. Your sisters are your personal life. Your work life didn't have anything to do with either. Now, it's all muddled." He smiled. "I asked around about you when Violet mentioned you."

She'd mentioned him to *Dennis*, her sponsor?

"Yeah, yeah." McCauley chuckled. "I got the skinny from your SWAT lieutenant. You know, he's my half-brother?"

Blake nodded.

"He couldn't have spoken more highly of you."

"Because he only told you the work stuff."

"Nope. Nothing held back, all of it. The full scoop. How do you think I knew about you compartmentalizing? Gage told me you work hard to keep it all separate."

"Fine." What was he supposed to say?

"I'm not trying to tick you off," McCauley said. "I'm trying to explain—badly, apparently—that when you work so hard to keep it all apart, the moment those walls crash down, it's twice as hard to deal with. You can't just flit from one thing to another. It's all mixed. People want to know what's going on with the other thing. Guys at the precinct will work out who your dad is."

"I never kept it a secret."

"And Violet will want to help you process all of it. Women love that stuff. They want to get you to talk about your *feelings*. You should hear my wife tell me I need to 'talk it out.'" McCauley snorted. "I do that with others so I don't need to do it with her. She doesn't need to hear all my garbage."

"Because you keep it all compartmentalized?" Sounded like the pot and the kettle were the same color, as well as being the same skin color.

McCauley grinned. "How do you think I recognized it right away?"

"So you've got me pegged. That it?"

"Takes one to know one. Isn't that the expression?"

Blake lowered his arms, rolled his shoulders, and tried to figure out how to get rid of the sensation of drowning. "Two bombs."

McCauley's brows rose. "Two?"

"My truck, which Violet was driving, and the front of the building. Probably the waiting area." They'd have to figure out what the guy carried in and left inside and also when he'd managed to wire up Blake's truck.

And why had it gone off before Violet even started driving?

"She nearly died today." More than one time, she'd almost lost her life. People had died in the explosion. Others were injured. The ER swarmed with people, a lot of them bandaged and bleeding.

McCauley said, "This is usually where I caution people to not fall back into old habits that they can't control in order to cope with the fear and pain, but not everyone has the same issues. Moderation comes in all shapes and sizes."

"Coffee and a laptop are all I need."

McCauley went to the nurses' desk and grabbed a backpack, then slid a laptop out. "What are you thinking?"

Blake had seen surveillance footage of the guy. "The bomber signed the visitor's log as Malik Henderson."

"And he somehow managed to get DNA for the same man at his house just to throw us off."

Blake shook his head. "I'm not so sure. He didn't just leave one sample; his DNA was all over that house. He lived there."

"A dead man?"

And one who looked nothing like the person he really was. If that was the logical conclusion, what did it even mean?

An identical twin who didn't look like the dead man anymore?

Plastic surgery?

It didn't make sense. But he knew someone who could figure it out. McCauley logged in, and Blake entered the case number. He had the sketch, but he needed the man's actual photo. They'd have to run it against the prison footage, which the warden had sent him minutes before the building had exploded.

He didn't even know if the warden was dead or alive.

Blake called Vanguard, hoping Simon Olson would pick up. The guy was a genius at computer stuff.

"Hey, I don't know anything new, okay?"

"You...what?" Blake frowned. "New about what?"

"When I get an update, I'll call you." Simon hung up.

Blake stared at the phone. "What was that about?"

"What do we need?"

"A way to compare everything about these two images." He put the original ID photo from decades ago up beside the prison surveillance image. "I need to know if there's a way to tell if this is the same man."

McCauley said, "I know a guy," and lifted his laptop up. "Leave it with me."

"Thanks, Cap."

"And go see your father."

THIRTY-ONE

"I don't wanna hear it." She'd already been poked and prodded, now Granny was doing the same about Blake. "He doesn't need me here, being needy. He needs to do his job and see his father."

Granny settled into a chair on the side of the bed, but the angle made it too painful for Violet to look at her.

Not while her head pounded like this.

She lay back on the bed, and the nurse—Amanda, who she knew well enough to ask her how her kid was—felt around her head with gloved fingers. Violet needed a shower, a couple of over-the-counter pain meds, and a nap to end all naps. After that she would see how she felt.

The nurse hit a sore spot.

Violet gasped.

"I'll let the doctor know you—"

"I don't want an MRI." Truthfully, she didn't want to face the fact she would probably be a baby about lying there and feeling hemmed in.

"Are you refusing medical treatment?"

"Amanda, you know I'm not going to do that. If I'm medically compromised, I can't work a paramedic shift."

Amanda's straight face remained, and her chin lifted slightly. "Then it's a good thing we have adequate professionals here. That way, you don't have to worry."

"You suck."

The nurse flashed a smile. "Rolling your eyes will hurt, so I suggest you don't. Meanwhile, I'll go talk to the other nurses about how paramedics make worse patients than doctors do."

Violet snorted. She wasn't going to tell Amanda not to talk to the other nurses. It was how they stayed sane, and they all knew the rules. Kind of like how everyone in the world used their phone to distract them from reality—necessary at times, but also a habit that turned into a crutch.

Which Violet needed right now.

She shifted enough to get her phone out of her pocket, grateful the warden had brought it to her in his office.

She blew out a breath, not knowing if he was alive or dead... How many people had died today? All of it was too much. Her phone was cracked, and that fact barely registered in light of everything else.

The screen turned on, and looked at the messages she had. Blake's sister Mercy had sent her a few texts. Violet managed to record a voice message and send it back.

"I'm in the ER, but it's just bumps and bruises. Blake is fine also. He's here but going to talk to his dad. If he doesn't answer the phone, it's because he's working, okay? We're okay."

Mercy messaged back, a regular text, just seconds later.

Ok, but r u guys dating now?

Violet blinked back hot tears at the single note of normalcy in the middle of all this. A chuckle bubbled up.

"Maybe we need a psychological evaluation."

Her father's voice washed through her.

She stiffened. "For me laughing at a text message from a friend of mine?" She couldn't give him an inch, or he'd take a mile, and she would end up on a seventy-two hour psych hold.

Though there were times in her life that would've felt like a needed break from the craziness, she wouldn't waste the time of medical staff like that.

"I'll be the one to determine your status." He strode toward her.

"And if I request a different doctor?" She could. He shouldn't be treating a family member, according to the regulations they all lived by. His personal connection to her could compromise his judgment.

Except her life wasn't in danger, and he probably didn't care enough to be compromised.

If he did feel something for her, he'd never shown it. But after her epic failure, it had seemed more like he was only interested in asking if things were succeeding. When she wasn't a massive embarrassment to him.

He shone a light in her eyes, and she winced.

He said, "With the busyness in here today, I doubt anyone else is available, even if you decided to kick up a fuss."

"Maybe you should go treat someone in more serious condition than me." Then she'd have time to cool down, get her feelings all buttoned up. The way he'd taught her to never give away any of her emotions.

To the point she wasn't sure he even had any feelings.

He stared at her. "Is it necessary for you to be so combative?"

Violet stared right back. Was there any feeling at all in

there? Or was she just back to wishing things could be different.

They were, with Blake. That could be more than enough —a gift from God because nothing else in her life was going to go right. He was like a glimmer of hope in the dark.

"Perhaps we can...have coffee."

She blinked. "What?"

He glanced at his mother. "All of us."

Granny said, "That would be nice, George."

He asked her what'd happened to her and didn't react at all when she mentioned the bomb explosion and the fact she'd blacked out. In fact, he treated her like any other patient with whom he had zero personal history.

She wasn't sure whether to be impressed by his professionalism...or hurt that he gave her nothing. "I just need something for my pounding head, and I'll clear out so another patient can use this room."

"Did I miss the part where you became a licensed doctor in the state of Washington?"

Violet pressed her lips together.

"I'll get the nurse to give you something."

"So I am good to go?"

Rather than answering her, he looked at Granny. "I'll have a list of things to watch for, but she's right that we do need the room, and she doesn't need to be admitted." Then he turned to her.

Violet was about to make a crack about "she" being right here.

"Don't be foolish. You've hit your head enough the past few days that you'll need to be extremely careful."

"Thanks, *Doctor* Anderson." He hadn't been a father back when she was a child. He'd only been a man raising a doctor of his own. She doubted he'd be a father to her in the future since she'd completely failed at that.

Commotion erupted in the hallway. Violet stiffened, all the fear and heart-pounding making her sweat suddenly, like a switch had been flipped. Someone ran past the door, toward the front. Glancing back behind them.

Then someone else.

Dennis had gone...

She didn't know where he was. But whatever was happening in the hallway, she hoped it wasn't bad. *Lord, You hold everything in Your hands.* She never would have imagined what had gone down in the last week. Had it been only a handful of days?

God had completely changed the trajectory of her personal life in one swoop. Maybe her professional life as well, considering she couldn't do her job until she healed, and it was too dangerous to be at the center.

That nap sounded good right now.

Or maybe Blake would come over when the case was done, and they could cuddle up and watch a movie.

Violet slid off the bed and went to look out the door. Dennis had his gun raised, and a teenage boy stared him down. "Nope. Raise those hands."

It was Drew from the center who'd accused Austin of stealing from him.

What was going on?

Drew didn't raise his hands. His lips shifted, as though a decision was being made behind those eyes.

Don't do it.

She didn't want Dennis to have to kill him in the hospital. All this violence needed to stop. "Drew, do what he said!" Violet shuffled down the hallway, passing a couple of people.

She ignored them and the way her legs wanted to give out. "Listen to him."

"Hands. Up."

Drew glanced at her, something dark like hatred in his eyes. Then he spun around and pushed out a door.

Dennis rushed after him.

The door clicked shut before she reached it. A gunshot echoed beyond the door. Violet gasped. She yanked the door handle.

Her dad's hand slammed the door. "What do you think you're doing?"

"Someone could be hurt!" That teen was someone she knew. Someone who should never look at her with that expression. He needed help.

"You could get yourself killed." Her dad's dark eyes crackled with fire in those tiny gold flecks. "And I think you've risked enough already today, haven't you?"

Someone slammed against the door on the other side.

She gritted her teeth. "They could be hurt."

His stalling her could mean the difference between life and death. She spotted the shift in him, and he opened the door.

Dennis fell through onto the ground. Blood covered his chest.

Violet screamed. "Drew, what did you do?"

THIRTY-TWO

"Thanks, Sergeant." Blake hung up the phone and stowed it in his front pocket. He'd updated Deerdan and been ordered to report to McCauley right after he spoke with his dad so he could get his orders from the captain while he was here.

His texts to Jasper had gone unanswered.

After that weird response from Simon at Vanguard, Blake couldn't fight off the fear that had sunk into his gut. There might be something going on that he wasn't privy to. But with the amount of things on his plate right now, he was just going to trust the people he knew.

Whatever it was, they would loop him in if he needed to know.

Maybe You could help with that, too. Seems like You could —since everyone says You're all powerful.

Now that he had decided it was true that a higher power existed, he had to make a choice.

Either pretend ignorance on the subject just so he could go his own way and keep doing whatever he wanted...

Or he could investigate it like a case. Depending on the

conclusion—the result—he would know what steps to take next.

He had plenty to pray for now, with all the people in his life. Violet. His family. Her family. The case. His work friends, former SWAT guys. Liam and his new life. Dakota and his second chance.

He could sit with a hot cup of coffee, pray for an hour, and still come up with more things to talk to God about. Sure, He probably already knew it all, but it made Blake feel better to say it.

To know God would have it all in His hands.

Like the way He had kept them alive so far. He prayed God would keep Violet from being too hurt as well.

In the hallway where his dad's room should be, he spotted a room number. The one he was looking for should be the next one. But where were the two officers who should be on the door?

Blake glanced around. Farther down the hall at the nurses' station, that looked like a kind of welcome desk, he saw a couple of nurses in scrubs working.

He knocked and let himself into the room, announcing, "Detective Reed."

But the room was empty.

The bed unmade.

He spun and strode to the nurses, flashing his badge. "The inmate in five-twenty. Where is he?"

The nurse looked over from her monitor screen to him. "The cops got a message that he was to be transferred. Some Captain...McCallar?"

"McCauley."

She nodded. "That's the one."

Blake didn't like the sound of this. "Transferred where?"

"Dunno." She shrugged. "But transport showed up, and the three of them got the inmate loaded up to go."

"How long ago?"

"Few minutes, maybe. You just missed them."

Way too odd, since McCauley hadn't said anything to Blake about moving his father somewhere else. "The person from transport, who was that?"

"Some new guy." She shrugged again. "I'd never seen him before, but he seemed nice."

Blake found the sketch of the bomber and showed it to her. "This guy?"

"Yeah, that's him..." Her voice trailed off. "Is he some kind of *bad guy?*" Her eyes glinted, and she gasped with extra interest on top. Her whole demeanor changed. "Is he *dangerous?*"

"Do everyone a favor. Don't go lookin' for trouble."

"What about lookin' for you? Can I do that?"

Blake turned and walked away.

"You could give me your number!"

He ignored her, found the elevator, and jabbed at the button. The display above the closed doors indicated it was on the ground floor. At this end of the building, the elevator would let out into an alcove with a door that went outside to the two-story parking structure that had been added to the building by a walkway.

This was taking too long.

He raced for the stairs and grabbed the rail as he sprinted down four flights, skidding around each landing and launching himself down each time.

His father was gone.

Two cops were taking him out, and the bomber was with them. Just a year and a half ago, a terror attack on this same hospital had been avoided because the bomb squad defused a device that was supposed to have torn the whole place apart.

The story would be quite different if Malik Henderson managed to fulfill the dream today of a group of domestic terrorists.

Blake tugged out his phone and called dispatch. He announced himself and said, "Possible bomb at the hospital."

The dispatcher actually gasped. "Another one?"

He didn't want to say it, but... "Yes. The bomber is here."

"Copy that. Sending backup and the bomb squad to your location and looping in hospital security now." She paused. "Oh. They're already en route. We have an officer down at your location."

Blake flinched, then dragged the door open. "Who?"

"Uncertain. It sounds like it might be multiple, but some of it is just body cam footage. There's backup on the way."

He spun around in the alcove between the door to the stairs, the door to outside, and the elevator, which beeped. The doors opened, then tried to close. It beeped again, blocked by something.

He gripped the phone and went to look. Two police officers lay on the floor of the elevator, the door blocked by one foot. No blood. How had they...

Blake shoved the door open and knelt near the first one. Checked a pulse. "Alive but knocked out. Maybe a stun gun?"

The other was alive also.

"Copy that. I've updated the notice."

Blake's heart sank at the reality of what had just happened and how the entire police force and the general public would see it. "We've got a prisoner escape on our hands."

"I'm sorry, Detective?"

He hit the emergency button to open the doors and hold

the elevator here, then stepped out. "Jamal Reed has escaped police custody. He's an inmate at the prison, and he was here following a stabbing."

Had the whole thing been planned?

Had his father lied to him for years? A long con wasn't exactly unheard of. He might've been playing all the angles he could get. For years. All for that one shot at freedom.

He'd had to get stabbed to pull it off.

But he'd done it.

Had that phone call been a moment of weakness? Guilt over what he was about to do?

Some of the hospital staff and a security guard rushed over from the hall.

"In there." Blake motioned to the elevator, then drew his weapon.

He pushed out the door to the parking lot and sprinted down the breezeway. Wind whipped through the open sides, whistling between posts and blowing ice-cold air at his face while he pounded the concrete.

On the far side, he punched through the door into the parking lot.

He searched, weapon raised, not quite sure what he'd do if he saw his father making an escape.

The bomber? He'd know exactly what to do.

He cleared two rows before he saw them at the end. One man dressed in scrubs, helping a man in a hospital gown into a car.

"Police! Hands up!" At least that part of his instincts stuck to what he was trained to do. The rest of it would be a crapshoot.

The gowned man stumbled against the car and cried out.

His father.

"Stop!"

The orderly drew a weapon.

Blake fired at him and dove to the ground, taking cover behind a car. "Lay your weapon down and surrender! It's over, Malik!" He needed to know who this guy was, but more whether he had hidden another bomb in the hospital before this—like he had with the prison.

And Blake's truck.

Was this his father's escape? If the bomb in his SUV had been meant for him, then Blake shouldn't be alive to see this.

Maybe he was supposed to be dead at the hands of this bomber.

He lifted his head enough to crane his neck and look over the back bumper. A shot pinged off the paint. Blake slumped back to the concrete with an "Oof."

One of them yelled, too far for him to hear what they were saying.

Then a car engine revved.

Blake scrambled up, gun raised, and watched the car speed away. *License plate.* He raced after it and got a few of the digits before all the strength seeped from him.

He stopped, bent forward, and tried to breathe.

They were gone.

THIRTY-THREE

"Drew Fullerton." Violet spotted Blake at the far end of the hospital staff kitchen, the spot this officer had chosen to take her statement about McCauley's shooting.

Blake came over and nodded to the officer in a suit, not a uniform. "Wilks." Then he touched her shoulder, leaned down, and kissed her. Short, sweet, and to the point.

"Reed." The way the older officer said it made Violet frown. "I'm interviewing this witness. She was there when McCauley was shot."

Not exactly what she'd said, but the look on Blake's face kept her mouth closed. His pain was more important than clarity. "What is it?"

His expression shuttered. "I called Gage. He was already on his way. They're brothers."

"I'm conducting an interview." Wilks stiffened and frowned at her. "You know this kid?"

Violet nodded. "Seventeen. He's a student at Freemont High, on the chess team."

A woman strode in wearing dress pants, flat shoes, and a

wool coat—a police shield tucked up on her coat collar. "Update."

Blake kept quiet, as though he'd already said everything he needed to, but he turned to include this woman in the conversation.

Detective Wilks said, "McCauley was shot and stabbed. Ms. Anderson here is the daughter of the chief of surgery, which is why she isn't in cuffs now as an accessory."

Violet stood up so fast the chair slid back. "Excuse me?"

The woman frowned at Wilks.

Blake shifted Violet behind him. "She isn't an accessory." He held his body stiffly. Violet laid a hand on his side, trying to reassure him, and spotted gravel dust on his pants. He'd been on the ground.

"What is going on?" she asked.

No one answered her.

The woman said, "McCauley was hit by the person who has been murdering our dealers."

Both Blake and the other cop flinched.

"Drew is the one?"

Blake slid over so she could move out from behind him. "Violet, do you know anything about Drew, or have you seen anything that might indicate he's a killer?"

She opened her mouth, about to object strongly. "I don't even know what that would look like. I'd never believe it of any of the kids. Drew? He isn't different from any of the others."

The woman said, "Could be a family member, or someone he's friends with. An older man. An accomplice." She stuck her hand out. "Sergeant Deerdan. Wilks' and Reed's boss."

"Sarge?" Blake shifted like he was nervous.

The woman shook her head. "You gave me your statement. Now we wait. The detectives from major crimes are checking surveillance. We need to know if he brought a bomb into the hospital before he broke your father out of custody."

"Wait..." Violet choked. "What?"

"Your boyfriend is an accomplice, just like you are," Wilks fired at her.

"Wilks, go back to the office and sign out. You're on suspension for two days."

"Sarge!"

"Get out of here." Deerdan folded her arms.

Wilks tossed his notepad on the table and huffed out. Her father came in as he exited. "Something I should know?"

Violet didn't actually want to talk to him, but if he had information her feelings didn't matter. "How is Captain McCauley?"

Blake squeezed her hand.

"I've just spoken with his family. His wounds are severe, but there's no reason why he shouldn't make a full recovery." Her father was every inch the surgeon, no emotion for the rest of the time, but right now, a hint of something empathetic slipped through a crack in his armor.

Violet said, "Thank you." Because he'd come here to tell her, and he'd shown her a little piece of the man he was on the inside.

"And while I was repairing the damage to your captain, Detective Reed allowed his father to escape police custody."

"Dad—"

The sergeant cut her off. "Considering hospital security is currently ensuring that an explosive device hasn't been planted in the hospital somewhere, about to go off and kill us all, perhaps we can avoid the accusations and rely on truth." She turned to Blake. "I've got a BOLO out on the license plate you got, one on Malik, one on your father, and another on the kid."

Violet spotted it.

An infinitesimal shift in her father no one else would've noticed. About what?

"Malik?"

He turned to her. "What?"

"That's what you reacted to."

He waved her off. "I've got work to—"

The sergeant got between him and his route to the door. "Doctor Anderson, I'd like to speak with you about your history regarding this case. It's just a chat."

Violet strode over to stand by Deerdan. "Do you know Malik Henderson?"

Blake did the same, showing her dad a photo. "This man?"

Her dad frowned. "That's not the guy I knew." He lifted his chin. Defensive.

"This image now is not the man you knew by that name?" She could read him better than anyone, and given the look on his face, he hated her for it.

Blake said, "I've been trying to figure out why no one recognizes him. Why Malik Henderson was declared dead and a man with a different face has his DNA. Do you know anything about it, Doc?"

Her father bristled.

"You used to do plastic surgery." Violet folded her arms despite the fact it was a serious leap. Maybe he went to high school with Malik, or they'd played basketball on the same court. She could be grasping at nothing, but she refused to let this go until they got to the bottom of it.

"My patients expect a level of anonymity. It's the law." He spat the words at her. "You, of all people in this room, should understand medical practice."

Sure, he followed the rules when it served his purpose.

The rest of the time, he remained the law unto himself.

Violet's stomach roiled. "Dad, what did you do?"

He barked a laugh. "That's rich, coming from you." He slapped his chest. "I didn't have a mental breakdown. I survived medical school, residency, and everything they threw at me. I didn't let it break me. I let it forge me into steel."

"So you threw it all at me, trying to do the same." Go figure, he thought he'd been doing her a favor. "Who is Malik Henderson to you?"

"I want my lawyer."

"You're not under arrest," Blake said.

Her dad grabbed her arm and dragged her away from Blake. "This is who you're choosing? His father is a criminal! A murderer!"

Uh, *yeah*, she was choosing Blake if he would have her. "And what are you?"

"It's guys like him that destroy the fabric of our society."

She didn't even know where to start with that. "You're hurting me."

"He probably let his father go. He's the one who should be arrested."

Blake dragged her father back, turned him around, and started to put cuffs on his wrists. All the words he'd said blurred in her mind but she heard *assault*. Tears rolled down her face.

Sergeant Deerdan squeezed her shoulder. "I'll take it from here."

"They forced me to operate on them. I didn't have another choice!" Her dad's words were muffled, his face against the wall. "They were going to kill my family if I didn't change their appearances so they could hide from the police."

Deerdan walked him out of the room.

Violet shuddered. "They?"

There was more than one person her father had

performed surgery on? And how did Drew factor into any of this? He'd killed people. And he'd nearly killed a man she cared for dearly.

Blake swept her up into his arms, lifting her to her tiptoes as he kissed her.

All the thoughts in her head eclipsed into nothing but the feel of him. His strong arms around her. The way he shuddered as she had, bleeding off the stress and fear. Finding solace in the comfort of each other in just one stolen moment.

Just as the kiss started to deepen, he tore his lips from hers and tucked his face in her neck. He held her tightly, and she did the same with him. Breathing. Thanking God quietly. As if she would ever believe that he'd been an accomplice to his father's escape.

"Reed!"

Blake turned, not letting go of her. A man she didn't know, but who was clearly a cop, stood in the doorway.

Blake said, "Lieutenant."

Great, another superior? She should go and check in with Granny and also Dennis's family—make sure they were all okay. "I should—"

The lieutenant said, "Bring her with you. You'll want her with you when you hear this, and I want to meet your girl."

THIRTY-FOUR

I want to meet your girl.

The words rang in Blake's head as they threaded their way through hospital hallways to the security office. "I figured I'd be getting suspended. Instead, you're inviting me to a meeting?"

Gage glanced back and winced. "Deerdan didn't want to make the call. Apparently, she likes you. Also, she's been wanting to knock Doctor Anderson down a peg or two for a while." He shrugged.

So, he was suspended. "How long?"

"Until your father has been apprehended and an Internal Affairs investigation clears you of any involvement. Officially."

Hmm. That meant Gage had something for him to do *unofficially.* "Sounds good."

Violet gasped. "What do you mean it sounds good? You just practically got fired!"

Gage grinned. "I like her."

Then he slipped into the security office.

Blake touched Violet's shoulder. "I won't be able to work for a while. You won't be able to work for a while."

Her eyes narrowed.

"That means we have time to date." He might be worried about his father, and helping where he could, but he could multitask. "How do you feel about tubing?"

"Like in the snow?"

He grinned. "Up in the mountains. You get on one of those inner tubes, and they push you down a hill."

"In the snow?"

He chuckled. "We can get hot cocoa after. And if you ask nicely, I'll warm you up." He tugged her close.

"Mr. Reed, I am a *lady* and as such—"

He kissed her because she was so cute. "I know." He squeezed her shoulders. "Maybe we could go to church as well. Find a study, or something that I can read so I can learn what it's all about."

Her smile widened. "That would be great."

He sighed with his face close to hers. "We should go see what my boss wants me to see."

"Well, he did just suspend you."

Blake drew her in for a hug, but all of her drew him in. Like that tube going over the crest of the hill and careening down the lane at high speed. Ice spraying his face. The rush. The laughter.

Hopefully, this ride never ended.

That's Your domain, I guess. So what do You say? Is this real?

Violet touched his cheeks. "Your father escaped. Mine just got arrested. Why am I happy?"

"Because life is good things and bad, all mixed together. You have to let the good lift you up so the bad doesn't drag you so far down that you can't get up."

The skin around her eyes flexed. "I'm ready for some good."

"Me, too."

They stepped together into the security office where he spotted one uniformed guard—one of the cops he had found in the elevator—and his lieutenant.

"You good?" he asked the cop.

The guy nodded from his chair but looked haggard. "My partner is getting an X-ray on his wrist."

Blake asked, "How did the prisoner seem?"

He hadn't even had the chance to talk to his father. It had been weeks, apart from the couple of phone calls.

The officer said, "Something was going on with him. We clocked it when he woke up from the surgery. He knew what was gonna happen. He was expecting it. That's how we didn't get killed. He grabbed for my stun gun before the other guy could kill us and knocked us out instead. I guess my partner pulled his gun. That's how his wrist got fractured."

Blake felt Violet's fingers entwine with his.

"I'm surprised the other guy didn't kill him for it. The whole thing seemed like an old grudge. As soon as the elevator doors shut, Reed was like, 'This isn't how this goes down. I told you that's not who I am anymore.'"

Blake needed to hear that.

"Then some other stuff like, 'There's no score to settle, Mal. You made the bomb, and I took the fall for it because I was dumb enough to get caught. We're done.'"

Blake's entire body tensed. His dad hadn't made that bomb.

Gage asked, "And the other guy?"

"He goes, 'You know what we have to do. He'll never let us go unless we end it.' And the prisoner was like, 'He already got rid of me when I took the fall for all of it.'" The officer shook his head. "Then the other guy went to kill my partner and me."

"That's all of it?" Blake needed to know.

When the officer nodded, Blake pushed out a breath and let go of Violet's hand. He paced the room and tried to process what that meant. "I can't believe you remembered it like that."

Blake nodded. "The DA must love you, recounting everything for the court."

The guy said, "Sorry we couldn't keep your dad safe."

Blake said aloud what he'd been hoping and praying since it happened. "He didn't leave of his own volition. He was abducted from police custody."

Gage said, "Either way, he's an inmate out loose, which launches a manhunt. But I've got Vanguard here on it. They have something happening right now, but there are enough operatives to spare, so we have a chance to find him before the feds do." Gage tipped his head to the side. "But the FBI and the US Marshals have been called, and the state police are spooling up."

"What do you want me to do?"

"Is there anywhere he might go where you'd think to look for him. I want a list of places you frequented together. Anywhere he might go to hide—like a cabin or a friend's place —and anywhere he'd stop to get money or other supplies. That's your job right now."

Blake said, "Because I'm suspended, so I can't help with the hunt."

"I don't like it any more than you do," Gage said. "You're part of my team, and that's the way it stays. But in this? Yeah, you take a step back."

"What about Drew?" They all turned to Violet. She blushed. "Is there any way I can help with him?"

"Unless you know where he'd go?"

Her face fell a little. "I don't know much about his personal life or where he lives. I saw a yearbook in his back-pack once. That's how I knew where he goes to school. Sorry."

Blake slid his arm around her shoulders. "We'll run him. Track him down. And hopefully, bring him in safely."

Gage's phone buzzed.

The officer who'd been dazed looked at the lieutenant. "Update?"

"The preliminary search of the hospital revealed no devices anywhere. They're doing another, more thorough, search now."

Everyone blew out a relieved breath.

"And we got Drew Fullerton's preliminary reports back. Parents are deceased. He was dumped in the foster system at a young age. Bounced around. Landed in a group home. Two officers paid one of the foster parents a visit. Apparently, he was friendly with an older gentleman who lived next door. African American, kept to himself, and liked to tinker with electronics in his garage. They moved a few years back but believe Drew kept in touch with him."

"And the house where we found Marco in the freezer?" Blake asked.

Gage nodded. "It's next door to the house they used to live in."

"That's the connection. The bomber lived next door." They needed to find Drew before he hurt anyone else. And his father and Malik before the feds took them out with long range rifles without asking any questions.

His father, who had taken the fall for all of it.

"Head out," Gage said to him. "Get me that list of places your father might've gone."

Blake nodded, and he and Violet stepped into the hallway.

She eyed him. "You okay?"

"The cops never believed my father worked alone, but he wouldn't name his co-conspirators. He just took the fall for all of it. If they were there, they were vaporized in the blast."

"They must've ditched him early enough for him to get away. Or they sent him in alone." She winced.

"He wasn't just in the wrong place at the wrong time. He was one of them. A man who wanted to put the hurt on a shipping magnate to try and change the course of society. He wanted the world to sit up and take notice."

Her expression softened. Even though she should want nothing to do with him, she was still here.

"And whoever they were working with—along with Malik—had your father change their appearances so they could continue to hide from the police."

"So, there's no way to know who the third man was or where to find him."

"Drew." Blake didn't like saying it, but unfortunately he was the key to this. "He's the weak link."

"You think they'll go after him?"

"Drew's the one who knows too much. A loose end they'll need to tie up." The way they might with his father. Though, it had sounded like Malik wanted his dad so they could get revenge together against the third man.

Lord, what is the truth here?

There were so many lives at stake. Whatever they did next, it had to be done with the minimal number of casualties.

They needed to save as many lives as possible.

THIRTY-FIVE

Malik pulled into the alley beside the house, all the way down to the garage. He'd left the door rolled up. As soon as they were out, he would roll it down so the car was out of sight.

The police would never figure out which house he was at. They'd be chasing their tails for days.

"Let's go." He didn't bother looking at Jamal. The guy was probably dead, he'd made so many groaning noises on the drive over. He probably had internal bleeding.

Instead of his old friend helping him, Malik would end up having to bury a body.

He'd get Drew to do it.

The kid would do anything for him. That was how their relationship worked. He'd read all the psychology books about codependent relationships and vulnerable adolescent brains. And how susceptible they were to suggestion.

It hadn't been difficult.

Shame that he couldn't do the same with Jamal.

Malik opened the passenger door. "Prison changed you."

"You thought it wouldn't?" He didn't move or even open his eyes.

"You'll freeze in that gown. I have clothes for you inside the house."

Jamal took forever to get out of the car while Malik held the door and waited. Even longer to get from the detached garage to the patio. Inside, he'd left the heater pumping.

"Bathroom is halfway down the hall. Don't fall, 'cause I ain't comin' in there to get you." Malik went to the coffeepot. "And don't bother lookin' for a phone because I've got the only one."

And it had been ringing off the hook, as everyone used to say when phones had a base and sat on the counter rather than now when it was a human requirement to be accessible twenty-four seven.

Malik poured two coffees.

Daniel hadn't let up for even a second. And somehow, Jamal thought he had it worse in prison? He didn't even know what they'd been through. What Malik had been through.

At least Jamal still looked like himself.

A stranger stared back at Malik in the mirror, and the scars had taken years to heal. He'd rather have split and landed in Costa Rica. Daniel would've killed him for running, and he said they should hide in plain sight where no one would expect.

He took his coffee to the living room, where he'd set up tables for constructing the devices he needed.

More perfect explosions. He liked to see them go off, but it wasn't always possible to be around to watch. He hadn't seen the prison go up. He'd been waiting across the street, waiting for the bomb Drew had planted under the seat in the truck to go off...but it hadn't exploded at the point the key was turned. Surprise, the kid screwed up again.

Since he hadn't called, Malik figured that was happening again.

Had he been arrested?

Malik's phone rang again, but he didn't answer Daniel's incoming call. Like he hadn't answered any of the other fifty.

"So, this is what you've been doing all these years?" Jamal shuffled in, tugged the chair over, and sat with a groan.

Malik got him a cup of coffee. "I figure we should celebrate you being a free man."

Jamal just stared at him.

"What?" They'd have to call the doc. Get Jamal the works, like Daniel and Malik had gotten, and make sure no one found him. Until then, he only needed to lay low. "You're free. You should be thanking me."

"I'm as free here as I was inside that prison, and at least there, I was able to share God's word and minister to the brothers."

"Share—" Malik sputtered. "Are you kidding me? You found religion? You're gonna get all high and mighty now and then try to turn yourself in? No." He waved both hands. "Forget about it. That's not happening. We take out Daniel. We make our final stand, and we go out on our terms."

It was why he'd done all this.

Daniel wanted the dealers taken out and the police distracted. It had been the perfect cover for breaking Jamal out of prison so his friend could help Malik take down Daniel.

Everything had gone according to plan, for the most part. But Drew was expendable. That was the point of having an accomplice.

After all, it was what Daniel had done to Jamal.

Malik should've let himself get caught by the police back then. Prison would've been better than the hell he'd lived in since that tanker exploded. No face. No name. No home. No peace.

Just Daniel and his orders. His master plan.

Malik was going to make sure this ended. The way it should have years ago.

Fire.

Death.

"My life is in His hands now." Jamal looked dead. His face was so serene.

Except that death never looked like that. It was ugly and bloody.

Jamal said, "Do what you will."

"I'll kill you."

"Then that is how I'll die."

The guy probably wanted to write a letter to his son or get ahold of the phone. No way would Jamal die without saying what he wanted to say. Malik was going to have to watch his back, or this Jesus Freak would turn him in.

"You're unbelievable." Malik shook his head so hard it thrummed with pain. A stress headache. He'd had them for years. "I have to work." He swore. "Just drink your coffee." He turned to his table. "We don't have long."

THIRTY-SIX

"You're sure this is it?" Blake didn't sound like he believed it.

"This is a crazy nice neighborhood." Violet looked at the house where they'd pulled over. A mansion lit up by solar lights in the flower beds. Manicured lawn. Cars out of sight rather than on the spacious driveway that circled around a fountain. "But it's the neighborhood someone tagged on social."

She'd tracked Austin down through his social media to a party and used the hashtag to trace the location from someone else in attendance.

"I guess we just circle until we see teens spilling out of a house."

Violet watched the houses on both sides as Blake drove down the street. "You know, I grew up in a house like this, and I can honestly say I have zero drive to spend so much money to get one now. What's the point? I'd just rattle around all the rooms and wonder why walking to the mailbox is so far."

Blake chuckled. "I think they drive by their mailboxes on

the way in. Or they hire someone to go get their mail for them."

"More money." She huffed. "You've got to get a house cleaner, a gardener, a guy to put gas in your car for you. Or drive you around everywhere. I'd rather pick my own produce at the grocery store than micromanage which lettuce I want with a personal shopper."

"You sure you didn't hit your head?"

"Oh, I hit my head." She had the splitting pain to go with it, even though the hospital gave her a pill before they left. "Maybe it jogged something loose. Hopefully, common sense."

She spotted a house that was lit up inside. Music loud enough to hear through the car windows. Vehicles of all kinds lined up and down the driveway.

Blake pulled over on the street in a space barely big enough for the car he'd borrowed. His had blown up, and the department one had blood on the back seat. One day, she'd drive her own car without fear of being blown up.

But it wasn't going to be anytime soon.

"Let's go roust some kids." Austin had just been released from jail. He was determined to party it up in his free time. Hopefully, he'd do the right thing and tell them what they needed to know.

If Drew was at the party, Blake had promised they would back off and call 911. Report a sighting of the kid the police were looking for—who Blake definitely *wasn't* looking for since he was on suspension.

They passed a few kids out front and headed inside. Violet blew out a tight breath at the volume of the music in here.

Blake glanced at her. "I'm good if you want to hang outside."

She shook her head. Neither of them needed to be alone right now. She knew he was worried about his father and wanted to help him do what he could to find Jamal.

And she'd been praying nonstop since she found out what happened.

Whether Jamal escaped of his own volition or Malik broke him out against his will, the feds were only concerned with getting him back. They had an escapee, a dangerous criminal, to hunt down and bring in.

By any means necessary.

"I want to stay with you."

His expression softened a fraction. He looked like he might kiss her, but two teen girls stepped into the entryway. The couple making out on the stairs didn't stop. Glass shattered, and several teens cheered. Was there even a legal adult in the house?

"What are you guys doin' here?" The first girl lifted her phone and snapped a photo of them.

"He can stay." The other grinned. "He's cute."

He's a cop. Violet held the words back, or there would be pandemonium at the party. "We're looking for a friend of mine. Austin Phelps. You know where he is?"

The first girl set a hand on her hip. "What you want him for?"

One thing would be a safe bet. "He's got somethin' for me, and I've got the cash to pay for it." And she knew how to not gawk at a house like this—because she'd grown up in one. "Find him for me. Maybe there's somethin' in it for you." She shrugged like she wasn't bothered either way.

"I'll find him." The second girl wanted the payday more. She rushed from the room.

The other one rolled her eyes, took another picture of them, and sauntered out.

Violet turned to Blake and spoke close to his ear so she didn't have to shout. "If she posts that and someone puts it together that I work at the center, they probably won't let me come back."

Volunteers who'd done less than that had been fired.

"And if it saves a life?"

She studied the question in his eyes. He held back his true opinion, maybe wondering if she wouldn't like it. "It's worth me losing my job and everything else if it saves a life."

"Let's hope it doesn't come to that."

What would she do if she had to find a new career? How did people figure that out?

Blake shifted. She turned to see Austin saunter in, wearing a pair of sweats with stripes down the sides, sneakers, and a tank top. His hair was mussed, and he tipped his head.

They all went outside.

He turned to them; his eyes glassy. "You think I wanna be seen talking to cops?"

"No, I don't," Blake said. "Which is why I'm here."

Austin flinched. "Huh?"

"I got suspended. I'm not a cop right now. I'm just here with Violet so she can ask you some questions."

That was her cue. Austin's face twisted, and he was gearing up to come at her with whatever he wanted to say. Before he could, she lifted a hand and started first. "Don't. We're looking for Drew. That's all."

"I don't have nothin' to do with him."

"Maybe so, but we need all the information we can get on him." He knew *something*. "If you know anything at all, tell us. We need to find Drew before he kills someone else."

Austin made a face. "So you know?"

Did that mean *he* knew? "Why didn't you tell someone?"

"I ain't a rat. And he'd probably have killed me." Austin sniffed.

Blake asked, "Where can we find him?"

"He always talks about this rich uncle he got himself. How he had all these toys 'cause the guy bought him whatever he wanted." Austin shrugged. "I ain't into that, so I didn't ask. If I need something, I get it myself." He pounded his chest with the flat of his hand.

"Where would he go if he needed to hide?" Violet bit her lip, her heart breaking more than it usually did when faced with reality. Some of the kids she knew were determined to self-destruct, and there was nothing anyone could say or do to change that.

"Said the guy had a cabin up off Markers Lane, up in the woods." Austin sniffed again.

"What about here in town?" No sense going on a wild goose chase, driving all over the mountains for what might turn out to be nothing.

"I don't keep tabs on him. I stay out of his way."

"What about the guys on the team? There any Freemont kids here?"

"Chess kids?" Austin snorted. "Nah. These are Eastown kids."

Great. Completely the wrong school, and they were football rivals. "Do you know any of his friends?"

Austin said, "If he has any."

That was as much as they were gonna get out of the kid. He'd shut down. Still, the center volunteer in her cared enough that there was more *she* wanted to say. But would he even listen?

Sometimes, she could say everything right, and still, the only thing left to do was watch the destruction happen.

"Thanks." Blake took a step back; her signal that he was ready to go.

"Get some help, Austin. Or you're gonna career down this path, and when you hit the bottom, there won't be a way to get back up."

But she would be praying for him.

"Come visit me in the joint when they lock me up." Austin chuckled, apparently finding his own joke amusing.

She didn't.

Blake snagged her hand. "Come on."

Violet sighed. "Was that even worth it?"

"It's a lead we can follow. Hopefully, we'll get an address on that cabin, and maybe he's there. We can pray no one is hurt, and the takedown is peaceful."

"We can."

He drew out his phone and made the call.

THIRTY-SEVEN

Blake's whole body tensed. His usual role would have him walking with the other SWAT team members toward the cabin. Right now, he couldn't do anything, not even run the drone.

The cabin was small enough that they didn't need the drone to go inside, so he'd shown Jasper's cover, Officer Baker, how to fly it around outside and get the data on heat signatures. They'd ascertained one person was inside. Lying down, so most likely sleeping.

Violet was in the front seat of his car with the door open so he could see her in the dark with the dome light on. Doing something on her phone. Safe. Out of the way. Kind of like he was supposed to be.

Except he couldn't wait back like a civilian and not watch his team breach this house.

He slid the earpiece in with the wire connected to his radio. He held it and watched like a scene commander as SWAT crept up to the house. Gage gave a hand signal, and two officers went around the back.

Where are you, Jasper? His friend hadn't answered any

calls. When the SWAT page went out, signaling an operation, he hadn't responded to that either. What on earth was going on with the guy?

Blake watched the front door breach and prayed for Jasper, even though he was angry the guy hadn't shown. He'd gone AWOL rather than being here for Blake.

Gage and whoever was with him stopped about six feet from the front door. "Green for entry."

"Copy that," came the reply from one of the two men at the back door. If there was a back door. If not, they'd watch windows from outside in case the man in the house jumped out.

The lieutenant ratcheted his shotgun and blew a hole in the door where the handle was. The door propelled in, wood splintered...

And nothing exploded.

Gage said, "Clear."

Then, the SWAT officers entered the house. They'd still have to be careful of trip wires and other explosives. But once entry had been gained, the chance the place was wired to explode dropped dramatically.

Blake tapped his free hand against the side of his leg, trying not to rush over there prematurely to look and wind up compromising the operation. Or getting himself or someone else killed.

He didn't turn but felt when Violet stopped beside him. "They're inside."

"Yes. It won't be long now."

Gage appeared at the door. "Violet! We need you in here!"

Blake set off at the same time she did. They jogged across the grassy dirt to the front door. He hung back so she could go in first, then said, "Got him?"

"This way." The officer led Violet through the cabin.

Gage shook his head. "Victim. She needs medical care."

Blake winced, striding back outside. "Where is he?"

"I can tell you he was here," Gage said, joining him on the porch. "Toothbrush. Razor and shaving cream. Some clothes in the drawers. This isn't where he always lived, but he came here frequently."

"And the victim?"

Gage said, "Early twenties. She's been here awhile."

Blake shook his head. "We need to find this guy."

The other two officers came around from the back. Gage said, "Find me something that tells me where he is."

"Yes, sir," the second man said as he ducked inside.

Blake paced the porch, trying to get a handle on the frustration. Violet was in there doing her job. Gage had jumped on his radio, calling in a medical chopper from the hospital. He could only stand here and...

Light flashed in the trees.

Then it was gone.

Blake didn't wonder what it was or what made that scant illumination. He just took off running.

The radio fell to the ground as he sprinted toward the trees.

Gage called out something.

Blake had his personal weapon in one hand and drew his penlight with the other. It didn't give him much light. The focused beam had little spread. But he got a look at the shadow moving ahead of him.

Gage ran up behind him. The guy was *fast*, so it was no surprise he'd caught up. "Go left."

That meant Gage would go right, and Blake would cut him off from the other flank. They'd close in and trap their prey between them.

"Benson PD!" Gage's voice sounded like thunder. "Drop your weapon and put your hands up!"

The figure stumbled and went down. A cry split the night.

Blake jogged close; his gun angled just in case the kid had a weapon. "Hands." Gage would have to make the arrest, but that didn't mean Blake wouldn't get a whole lot of satisfaction out of observing. "Don't move."

Drew gripped his ankle, wincing. Dressed in shorts with no shirt, the kid had to be freezing. Man-size whimpers came from his mouth.

Gage said, "Get up."

"I can't walk."

"Guess what you're gonna do?" Gage grabbed his elbow and hauled the kid up. "Hands behind your back." He arrested Drew on suspicion of committing multiple murders and read him his rights, then marched him back to the cabin.

"Who is the girl?"

"I'm not saying nothin'." Drew huffed. "You said I can have a lawyer."

"That I did," Gage said.

But Gage didn't offer one, and technically, Drew hadn't asked. If he said anything between here and the police station that would be up to him.

A helicopter crested the hill and landed between the cars and the cabin in the middle of the clearing.

Violet jogged out and met the medics. They ran into the house, and she came over, giving Drew a wide berth. "I'm going to go with her."

Blake nodded. "Good idea."

She hesitated for a second, then kissed him. "See you later."

"Yes, you will." She hurried away, and he turned to see Gage looking at him. "What?"

"Nothing," Gage said. "Clare still needs to call me back, but there might be a job opening at Vanguard if Violet is interested."

"Doing what?"

"They're in the market for an in-house medic." Gage shrugged. "I suggested Violet after meeting her, but Trey had already put her name in the hat. Says she's his best paramedic."

"Of course she is."

Gage grinned.

The helicopter took off a few minutes later, and when the wind and the sound died down, they all gathered around Drew. The teen shivered.

"Guess the kid's cold," Blake said to no one in particular.

"I didn't see any blankets inside," Officer Baker said. "Just a victim who will never be the same after this."

Drew said nothing. He just shivered and sniffed.

"This is where you give us something," Gage said. "Get yourself a deal."

"I'm not telling you anything."

"Fine. We've got plenty here. Your DNA, right? Or are you just the caretaker who makes sure she doesn't escape? You don't get to *touch*."

"She's mine!" Drew spat the words.

Another nail in his coffin.

"Where's Malik?" Gage paused for half a second. "What's he planning?"

Drew gaped. "You think I know where he is?"

"Yeah, we do," Blake said.

"If I tell you, you'll bust in and kill him."

"Like we should've done with you?" Blake wanted to throttle the kid right now, even if he wasn't legally an adult.

"You shot and stabbed a police captain." Maybe Drew believed he'd succeeded in killing McCauley.

"I know what happens to guys like me in prison. Maybe I wanna die here."

"That's not gonna happen," Gage said.

"If you want protection in prison, you blew your shot." Blake could've asked his father to look out for the kid. Even if he was a murderer, that didn't mean he couldn't turn his life around.

If Blake was worthy of redemption, then everyone else was as well.

He'd been on a rooftop, joking around with a couple of buddies, when he shoved one of the kids. All of them busted up laughing. Three twelve-year-olds hadn't known what to do when the kid took a couple of steps back—still laughing—and tripped. He'd sailed over the edge in a split second.

Gone forever.

They'd heard the sickening thud. The car horn.

And then they'd run for it. Never spoke of it again, just tried to pretend it never happened when the news reported the kid had jumped. Committed suicide.

If Blake could find redemption after that? Not as a cop. Anything he tried to do wasn't good enough. It didn't erase his responsibility for what happened, even if it'd been an acci-dent. He would always have that blood on his hands.

"I killed someone once." The words were out before Blake realized what was happening. "We were messing around on a roof, and he fell. We all ran, but I can remember the sound when he hit the ground."

Drew stared at him.

"It was an accident, but I've paid for it every day of my life since then. Thinking I was just like my father. That I should be in jail, too."

No one moved or said anything.

"But guys like you should be in prison because you take life and don't care. It means nothing to you." Was Drew a psychopath? Or was he just a kid influenced by a charismatic person he looked up to? "I hope you get everything you deserve."

Blake tried to sound like he was sickened.

It seemed to work because Drew said, "I didn't want to! He told me I had to do it."

Bingo.

"I don't believe you." Blake took half a step closer. "I think you liked it the same way you liked what you had in there." He motioned to the cabin, knowing the kid would understand he was referencing the girl he'd had captive. "You're sick. I think you did want to do it."

"I'm the victim here!"

"Right." Blake nodded, as if he'd actually believe that. This kid was nuts.

He'd rather be at the hospital with Violet right now. That would be far better than staring down this shivering teen who'd taken so many lives.

"He told me I had to! He didn't give me a choice."

"So let us take him down," Blake said. "Then he has no power to force you to do anything."

"I don't want him in prison with me! I don't wanna be anywhere near him."

"Malik—"

Drew cut him off. "Don't say his name." He was crying now. "I don't wanna hear it. He's sick. Nothing's ever good enough. You don't know what he's like."

Blake didn't care, either. He just wanted one thing. "Where is he?"

"I don't know!"

"How do you contact him?"

"I call his number. He doesn't like text."

Blake said, "Where's your phone?"

"I dropped it in the tunnel. It's in the water."

Baker said, "I'll get it," and raced to the house, on the hunt for how Drew got out of the cabin.

He had to have been in the tunnel before they even breached the place.

Gage squeezed Blake's shoulder. "Ready for phase two?"

"The part where we get him to call the guy and draw him out?"

Drew gasped. "I'm not doing that."

"You will if you want this to end," Blake said. "It will never be over if we don't take him down. Like Jamal, who thought he was out, but Malik kidnapped him from police custody."

What the kid said next would indicate whether that assumption was true.

Drew flinched. "Who cares about Jamal?"

Blake asked, "What do you mean?"

"He's just a diversion from the real plan."

THIRTY-EIGHT

Three days later

Violet padded on bare feet down the carpet of the hallway. The new black dress felt odd. If only she could be wearing something shorter for a date somewhere nice, but Blake had told her that was for this weekend.

She carried her heels in one hand, her clutch purse in the other.

Blake stood in her living room, wearing his dress uniform, gloves, and hat. He had her wool coat in his hands.

He stared at the headline of the newspaper on the end table. Above the fold it read "Beloved Police Captain Murdered." Most of the news coverage had been about how hospitals were supposed to be safe places, but it wasn't like the staff could've anticipated the influx of people from the bombing, a prison break, and a murder in one day.

Drew had told the police that Malik ordered him to kill McCauley as a distraction so he could get Jamal out the back.

All so they could enact some plan in which Jamal was the patsy.

No one had any idea what it was.

She walked right up to Blake and held his hand to steady herself while she slipped on her shoes.

"You look beautiful." He helped her put on her coat.

She turned to him, tugging her hair out of the collar, and then laid her hands on his shoulders. "You're pretty handsome yourself."

His smile had a tightness to it.

"You haven't called Jasper?"

"Let's go. I don't want to be late."

He was still suspended, but they both wanted to be there for support. Whether something went down today or not, it was important they show.

She watched him as he drove. "It's not good to let it fester. It'll eat at you."

"Maybe it should eat at *him*."

"You think it isn't?" Violet touched his knee. "There was nothing you could have done. Vanguard had it handled. If he'd told you that rebels had kidnaped Destiny and her friend at the mission center, you'd have jumped on a plane. By the time you arrived, the whole situation would've been over."

His nose flexed. A shrug of his mouth.

Not an agreement, but not a disagreement, either.

"They got her back. She's safe."

"Whether she's in one piece remains to be seen." He gripped the steering wheel. "He should've told me. Someone at Vanguard should've called me." He shook his head. "Simon thought I knew, I guess."

"She'll be home soon."

"Not soon enough," Blake said. "Their kidnap and ransom team got her back, but they need to 'debrief' her. Then they'll make sure she gets medical treatment and transport back. It's a remote area, so it could be a week."

She squeezed his knee. "I didn't even know Vanguard had a kidnap and ransom department."

"It's a team, I guess. All women. They call them the Famous Ones, whatever that means."

"I'm sure we'll get to meet them, and we can thank them for saving her life." The other woman Destiny had been kidnapped with hadn't been so fortunate. Her parents were grieving her tonight.

Destiny would be home soon with her family, and it would be all about recovery for her.

"I don't know anything about any of it. I'm not some international private security guy. I'm a local cop. Kind of above my pay grade."

"Then I'm glad they were there to help."

"Me, too." Blake groaned. "Ugh, I'm gonna have to apologize for yelling at Jasper."

Violet said, "Seems like he really cares for her."

"I yelled about that as well." He shook his head. "I should've been nicer."

"He knows you care about her. And nothing is going to wreck your friendship."

"I nearly might've." He parked in the packed lot at the church. A crowd dressed all in black—or police dress uniform—headed inside.

"Tell me again why they think this is gonna work." Violet had heard the whole plan and still couldn't see how they figured this was the most likely scenario.

"McCauley was targeted specifically. Drew had a photo of him on his phone."

"And the PD thinks that Malik will hit the funeral?" She bit her lip. "Why not cancel it and keep everyone from being in danger?" If there was a bomb threat, they shouldn't be here.

She had been having nightmares of the prison exploding. And the car, and her attack at the center. It had been so rough at one point she'd called Blake, and he'd been awake with the same thing. They'd talked for an hour until she fell back asleep.

"We need to capture him. There will be feds, cops, bomb techs, and everyone else inside."

"It'll be a closed casket, right?" Violet asked. "I mean, it's not like there's a body. He wouldn't even look dead." She twisted in her seat to face Blake. "Will he have makeup on so he looks dead, like people do on Halloween?"

Blake laughed quietly. "Come on or we'll be late for the action."

She was only allowed to go so that it would look realistic as an actual funeral for the fallen police captain, who'd reportedly taken a turn hours after surgery. Some kind of aneurysm that surprised the doctors and caused Dennis's sudden death.

At least his kids weren't little. Apparently, his adult daughters were excited to wail over their father like pro actresses, and he was going to take them out to get milkshakes after—something he'd done back when they were teens.

They headed in the front doors, and Violet drew on some of the deep conversations with McCauley she'd had over the years that he'd been her sponsor. If she did lose him, it would devastate her. She remembered the fear she'd felt at the hospital when he was bleeding in front of her.

Soon enough, tears rolled down her face.

She stood in the center aisle and stared at the closed casket.

Blake slid his arms around her from behind and laid his

chin on her shoulder. After a moment of silence, standing together like that, he said, "Let's sit."

They took an empty spot on a pew. A couple—a cop and a civilian like her and Blake—eased down the row to sit by them. She glanced over. It was Gage and probably his wife.

"This is Clare. She's the CEO at Vanguard."

A gorgeous dark-haired woman leaned forward. "Hi, Violet. I'd love to chat later if you have time?"

"Uh, sure. That sounds good."

Blake squeezed her knee that she'd crossed over the other. She was being folded into his life, and it was good. Granny had a life of her own, and Violet loved spending time with her, but having people her own age? A life outside of work where she wasn't trying to save lives and she could be appreciated for who she was?

She leaned over and kissed Blake on the cheek.

She then spotted Jasper over his shoulder, beside an older man in a fancy suit. It was Senator Hollingsworth.

Jasper said, "B."

He unfolded out of the pew and held out his hand. "Jas."

They shook.

Senator Hollingsworth said, "Is that what they call you? *Jas*?" He huffed. "I'm getting a seat." He strode away.

Jasper let out a breath he'd been holding. "You guys got room for one more?"

They all scooted down, and Jasper sat by the aisle. "I'm sorry."

Blake said, "Me, too."

A white guy and a blonde woman appeared by the aisle. "'Scuse us." The woman went first, easing by their knees to sit on Clare's side.

Blake said, "That's Roxie."

She whirled around so fast she nearly fell, her attention zeroed in on Violet. "This is Violet?"

"Yeah, it is."

Roxie squeezed her hand. "After. We *talk*."

Violet just stared at her.

"Roxie doesn't bite," Blake said after her as the woman eased down to sit by Clare, and they started talking.

The guy looked like Conrad, who worked at Backdraft Bar and Grill. "I'm Liam." He grinned while she shook his hand and just stood there holding it.

"Go sit down, bro."

"Right." Liam let go of her hand and went to sit on the other side of Roxie.

The pastor moved to the podium. "Welcome, everyone. Thank you for coming out on this cold day to honor the life of a man who warmed everyone he knew with light and hope. Who brought joy to so many. Captain Dennis McCauley—"

A muffled thud came from inside the coffin.

Violet shifted to get a better look.

The lid opened, and Jamal Reed sat up, wearing a trench coat. He looked around, blinking at the crowd of people.

Someone screamed, "He's got a gun!"

THIRTY-NINE

Blake got a look at the man's face. *His father.* He scrambled out of his seat while the room erupted into screaming and a rush of movement. There weren't many civilians in the room—and even less who were untrained.

"Move." He levered himself on the back of the pew in front of him and clambered over Jasper. "Everyone back."

Sergeant Deerdan called out, "Detective Reed, you're on suspension."

"So fire me." He strode down the aisle. "Dad!"

The room quieted a little, but not by much. He wound between a couple of people going in the opposite direction to get out. He didn't blame them, whoever they were. He didn't focus on their faces long enough to identify anyone.

"No one shoots!" He'd seen the look on his father's face.

Everyone in this room was armed.

He shoved down a nearby forearm. "Lower that weapon."

Three velvet steps up to the podium and the raised coffin that should've remained closed. No one had expected this.

"Dad!"

His father was sitting up with the gun in his hand. Trench coat on. Why would his father be wearing a trench coat?

Blake moved in front of officers with their weapons trained on his father. "No one shoots."

All his instincts were screaming.

This wasn't supposed to have happened.

"Dad!"

His father flinched. The gun seemed limp in his hand—or the hand itself wasn't exactly gripping the weapon.

His dad shifted his forearm on the edge of the coffin. His gaze darted around like he didn't know where to focus—or couldn't.

Jamal twisted, and the gun moved with him.

Blake got in front of his dad. "He has no idea where he is! Everybody chill!"

He couldn't watch his father be gunned down in front of him.

Not here.

Not today.

God, help us.

"We got you, B." That was Jasper, behind him to his left.

"Right here." Gage was to his right.

"Not gonna let you down." Liam.

His boys. His family in SWAT, here now and backing him up.

"No one shoots him!" He knew what he was asking—a lot. But Blake would let himself get shot before he allowed anyone to kill his father when it was so obvious that he had no idea what was happening.

"Dad." Blake kept moving.

"Hold up," Gage said. "Look at his chest."

Blake eased to the right in big side steps so he could see

between the lapels of the trench coat. "He's strapped." The move put him in the line of fire, but he didn't care.

"Son?" His father fought to focus.

Blake took a step closer. If his dad twitched his finger, he would likely fire and kill Blake.

A rush of boots seemed to hit like a wave crashing. "Federal agents!"

"Drop the weapon!"

"Drop it!"

Blake grabbed his dad's wrist, lifting the gun so it pointed at the ceiling.

"Bomb!" Gage's yell cut through all the noise. "Everyone *out!*"

He ignored it all and focused on his father. "I've got you. Just hold still."

His father had started to panic, shifting his legs in the coffin. Blake couldn't imagine how he'd feel if he woke up in a sealed box with no idea where he was.

"Give me..." He let out a sharp breath, realizing why his father hadn't simply dropped the gun. Why his grip had seemed limp, but the weapon stayed where it was. "This gun is glued to his hand!"

Blake got his hand around it, released the magazine and the bullet from the chamber, and tossed both on the floor to one side. "Everyone relax."

"We have to get out of here," Gage said. "I know that's the last thing you want to do, but the bomb squad is already here. Let them do their job."

Blake shook his head.

No way was he leaving his dad right now.

"Look at him." Blake still had a hold on his father's wrist. "He has no idea what's going on."

"We can work with this." Captain Espinoza stood behind

him, given the direction the voice came from. "But I need one second, Blake. So set his arm down and take two steps back. Make sure he focuses on you and doesn't move."

Blake didn't move.

"Come on, B." Jasper and he had settled things, and as long as Destiny got home in one piece, that would continue.

The rest, they would figure out.

Blake set his dad's arm down in the coffin. He didn't want to, but he took a step back. "Dad."

Another.

"I'm right here. Everything is going to be fine."

Captain Espinoza reached around and slid a body cam onto the front of Blake's jacket. "Get me a view on that device."

Okay, that meant being close enough to his dad that the bomb squad could see the detail. He could do that. "Got it." There was just one thing. "Violet, you still here?"

"Yes!" Thankfully, her voice sounded far away, like she was on the other side of the room.

"You need to go outside."

"I'm not leaving. Roxie, Clare, and I are staying right here."

"All of you are going outside!" That came from Gage.

"I know you didn't just tell me what to do, Gage Deluca."

The lieutenant said, "Woman, you are having my baby. Go outside, away from the bomb."

"So this child growing in me has to go without a father?"

Gage said nothing.

Liam tried. "Roxie..." He said her name like a moan.

"The three of us are going outside," Roxie said. "Where you won't have to worry about us."

Blake let out a breath. "Lettie!"

"Yeah?" She didn't sound happy.

"I love you."

Jasper shifted to his left. "Bro, it's been like a week."

"You weren't there," Blake said. "So you don't know."

He kept all his attention on his father, praying the bomb didn't go off until the innocents in the room were clear. He moved closer to the coffin.

"Okay, but I get it," Jasper said in a low voice.

Violet called out, "I love you, too, in case you're wondering."

Someone chuckled, maybe Espinoza.

Roxie said, "Lee."

"I know," was his reply.

"Forever, Clare," Gage said.

She said, "Always."

Captain Espinoza said, "Now that's all out of the way. Can we focus on the explosive device? The rest of you should clear out with the women. Blake and I can get this taken care of."

Blake stepped to the right so his hip touched the coffin. He reached over and widened the lapels of his father's trench coat. "Everything is going to be okay, Pops."

"Son."

Blake squeezed the side of his dad's neck. "I'm right here."

"Don't move." Espinoza snapped the order.

He held his father's hazy attention and prayed the fire captain knew what he was doing. That everyone would be safe and no one would be hurt.

You can do that. I know You can. I believe. Show us what to do.

If they survived, there was no way around it—his father would go back to prison. Whether breaking out was his choice or not he likely wasn't going to get parole. He'd be in there forever as an accomplice to all this. A dangerous criminal.

A guy who'd made bad choices.

But also a guy who had turned his life around and believed in God.

They were the same in all the ways that counted.

"I'm not going anywhere," Blake whispered.

Jamal's eyes warmed with what should've been a smile, but it was like his lips didn't know how to do that. "Love you. B."

Blake's eyes burned with hot tears. "Love you, too, Pops."

"There's a trigger somewhere," Captain Espinoza called it out loudly enough that Blake flinched. "This device has a trigger, and it has to be within range of a Bluetooth connection." Then he said, "We need to secure the mechanism. Then, we can disconnect the vest."

The guy was right—this was a suicide vest.

His father was an innocent victim.

He might've participated in a plot all those years ago and taken the fall for three men. All that responsibility lay on his shoulders. But he hadn't continued to make evil choices that hurt people.

Why did you blow that tanker, Pops? He'd always wanted to ask.

But that was a question a son would ask and he needed to be a cop right now. In case they didn't make it.

"Dad." He waited a second for his father to focus. "Where is Malik?"

He also needed to know who the third man was. Who else had been a part of their original plot? This was about more than just the two men. But they'd have to take them down one at a time.

His father shifted.

"Stay still." They didn't want this bomb to go off accidentally.

"Malik." His dad's brow furrowed.

"Where is Malik, Pops?"

His father hesitated. Then he said, "Here."

FORTY

"How do you do it?" Violet stared at the closed door to the church, standing in an ocean of police and firefighters. First responders of all kinds. She couldn't believe Jamal had sat up in the coffin, a gun in his hand, and a bomb strapped to his chest.

Clare and Roxie led her away.

Roxie said, "He must've drugged Jamal and figured out how to get him in there."

Clare nodded. "We need to talk to all the funeral home employees—"

"I thought we vetted them all." Roxie sounded insulted.

"My guess? He paid someone to put Jamal in that coffin." Clare's expression darkened. "He was going to kill us all."

But it hadn't worked. Even so, Violet couldn't relax. The danger wasn't over, yet. "How do you deal with it when they could die at any moment?"

Roxie said, "Work with them?" She rolled her shoulders as though antsy to be inside the church. "When he doesn't kick me out. Although, that's about covering Clare more than Liam not wanting me in the line of fire." She dug in her purse and pulled out an official-looking badge, slipping it onto the lapel of her coat.

Could Violet get to the place where she could work with Blake? She usually dealt with the aftermath of the incident, whatever it was. Not usually present for the entire thing. Being a paramedic was about getting the patient to the hospital. Keeping them alive long enough that the doctors and nurses could figure out how to save them.

All she did was bandage a person's wounds and rush them to the hospital.

She didn't know how to do the waiting.

Or solve a case.

Everything she'd tried hadn't worked. Except being a paramedic. But did that fulfill all she wanted to be in the world?

What am I supposed to be doing, Lord? She'd have to talk to Him about it—later.

Clare said, "Pray a lot." She ran a hand over her abdomen.

They'd made the right decision to come outside. After all, they were protecting an innocent life.

"And then work your angle."

Violet turned to face Clare. "You do...what?"

The Vanguard CEO smiled. "Attack the problem from another angle." She glanced around. "I've just got to figure out what it is."

Drew had been arrested. Jamal was inside, the victim of an attack planned by Malik. "The man who put Blake's father in that coffin is still out there."

Roxie stepped closer to them like she would cover them personally if something happened. "I'm thinking he's still out *here.*"

Violet gasped. "I don't do this stuff. I have no idea how."

"We know," Clare said. "We'll work our angle; you work yours, right?"

Violet shrugged. "I don't know what that is."

"How about working with Vanguard, my private security and investigation company, as our in-house medic." Clare seemed earnest. "What do you say?"

Was Clare trying to distract her? Maybe she thought it was better for Violet to think about something else. She bit her lip. "We should talk about it."

Clare squeezed her shoulder.

"I don't like waiting." Violet should pray, but the words wouldn't come. Maybe she should call Granny and check in. She pulled out her phone.

Roxie stayed her hand. "Don't use it. You could interrupt a wireless signal."

"What's the latest?" a woman called out the question.

They all turned, and Violet spotted her. "That's Sergeant Deerdan, Blake's boss at Intelligence."

Clare motioned the woman over and stuck out her hand. "Megan."

"Clare." She shook hands with the blonde. "Roxie."

"Meg."

Megan looked at Violet. "You hanging in there?"

Violet nodded, not sure how she felt about this woman and the way she did her job. Not knowing enough about the police department and how things operated meant it was hard to make a judgment call about the kind of cop—or boss—this woman was.

The front door of the church opened, and the guys walked out. Violet nearly sank to the ground in relief to see Blake and all his friends. But she was the only one about to collapse. The women with her stood without faltering.

How did they do that?

Cops swarmed the group, helping Jamal out since he couldn't seem to move under his own steam. He was all right. Even if he had to go back to jail, at least Blake hadn't lost him.

She started to go toward them so she could see how Blake was doing.

Roxie and Clare both closed in.

Clare said, "Hang back. Give them a second."

Roxie said, "He'll come to you, but let him do his job first."

Violet watched, shifting her weight from one foot to the other. She didn't even know that! Blake needed to explain it all to her so she didn't make a fool of him by doing or saying something the girlfriend of a detective shouldn't.

"I'll let them know you're all over here." Megan squeezed her shoulder and threaded through the crowd.

Violet pushed out a heavy breath, so relieved she couldn't even put it into words. But where was Malik? The police needed to arrest him for what he'd done. Someone should weave through the crowd, looking at every face and trying to find him.

If he was here.

If he wasn't, then none of this made sense. No one would believe Jamal did this to kill himself in an elaborate plot.

She backed up a couple of steps and turned, scanning the crowd. Malik was here. Surely.

As if she could do anything to help. She wasn't a cop. She was barely a paramedic right now.

Lord, why does it feel like You gave me so much, but it also cost about everything I had to give?

At the edge of the crowd, under a tree on the opposite side of the street, she saw a lone man watching.

A man she recognized from the prison waiting area.

"That's him." She grabbed Roxie's arm since Clare was pregnant. "That's Malik, the bomb maker."

Roxie grabbed the arm of a uniformed cop with a lot of bars on his sleeves and said something to him. Violet couldn't make out the words with the rushing in her ears. She was so mad she wanted to storm over there and...kick his shins. What else could she do?

Blake had nearly lost his father because of this guy.

Violet took two steps, and Clare had her arm.

"Not so fast," the Vanguard CEO said. "We hang back."

But it seemed like Clare wanted to watch what happened.

Roxie had a gun out and jogged across the street. "Malik Henderson, you're under arrest."

A crowd of cops followed her, backing up Roxie.

The guy by the tree hammered the button on a small black device in his hands. The cops threw him to the ground, and he screamed, yelling about how he had to do it. He had no choice. How unfair this was.

Violet and Clare stood on the sidewalk, close to the curb. Traffic had been nonexistent, but now a trail of trucks and SUVs sped down the street toward them. "What is—"

A window rolled down. Multiple windows.

The barrel of a rifle appeared.

Clare screamed, "Gun!"

The whole crowd reacted.

The train of vehicles sped up. Shots erupted from each one, a steady *rat-tat* of bullets flying into the crowd of cops and funeral attendants.

Clare.

She had her gun out, firing it at the lead vehicle.

But it was heading right for them. While everyone else dove for cover and people screamed, Clare stood her ground.

She was going to get killed.

Gage ran for them. "Clare!" He roared her name across the crowd.

Violet didn't think about what she was going to do. She just ran for the other woman and slammed into her.

Fire tore through Violet, like she'd torn something loose deep inside her.

She dragged Clare to the ground at the same time that Clare seemed to fold like she'd crouched at the same time intentionally. Violet's mind couldn't make sense of any of it. The two of them landed in a heap, Violet covering Clare with her body. She couldn't breathe. Every inhale burned like fire in her chest.

Clare continued to fire her gun with her arm around Violet.

The sound of all the gunshots was deafening.

She didn't...

She couldn't...

Screaming. Yelling. Gunshots. Engines revved, then died down. The smell—like hot engine oil and metal. Sulfur.

Clare shifted her. "Why did you do that? I was about to... Violet?"

She rolled to her back and pain exploded in her center from the movement. She gasped. The sky above was too bright. It hurt to look at.

Her eyes rolled back in her head.

No. She didn't want to lose consciousness. *Blake.*

Clare's face swam into view above her. "Blake!"

Her scream was swallowed up in all the screaming, the noise. The yelling.

The aftermath of a massacre.

FORTY-ONE

"Dad?" Blake gripped his father's upper arms. The old man had tackled him and been hit by a bullet on the way down.

He shifted his dad off him so his dad could lie on his back on the gravel. "Medic!"

So many others screamed from spots all over the parking lot and the grass around it. Yelling. Crying. It was like an ocean of grief.

In the distance, sirens broke through everything.

Help was coming.

"Hang on, Dad." There was so much blood on his father's chest. Where was it coming from? "Help is coming." He didn't know what to do. But Violet would. "Lettie!"

Where was she?

He'd been satisfied with the result in the church. They'd defused the bomb—and the situation. His father had been safely taken back into custody with no loss of life.

And now this.

Blake gasped. "Dad."

Jamal's eyes flickered. "Son."

"Hang on."

The momentary clarity in his father's eyes dissipated. "So many gifts."

"What are you talking about?"

His father's breathing grew shallow. "God gives me." His gaze drifted to the sky. "Free. My son." His fingers found Blake's hands. "This."

Blake swiped at the wet on his face. "You saved my life."

When the shooting started and everyone took cover, Blake had been looking for Violet. Gage had started running.

And then his father stepped in front of him and took the bullet meant for Blake.

"So many gifts." His father exhaled and his head slumped to the side. His eyes unseeing.

"Pop." He shook his father's chest. But it was no use. The old man was gone.

Blake leaned down and touched his forehead to his father's. "Love you, Pop."

Then he lifted to sit back on his heels. Feeling the burn of the crouch. His legs were losing feeling.

He stumbled to his behind and looked around where cops had started to get up. Liam was ordering people around.

Captain Espinoza jogged to his firefighters, who were starting to carry people.

Two ambulances rounded the corner at the end of the street, followed by a third.

Gage scrambled over someone and wound between two people to get where he was going. The crowd parted, and Blake saw him land beside Clare, taking her into his arms.

Where was Violet?

Gage shifted. He lifted someone else into his arms and stood.

"Violet!" He touched his father's chest one last time, then jumped up and ran for her.

He slammed into Jasper at one point, and they gripped each other's arms for a second. "I'll take care of your father."

Blake asked, "And yours?"

"Unscathed." His tone sounded like *surprise, surprise.* But Jasper passed him, and Blake continued.

He caught up to Gage at the ambulance. "Violet!"

Clare said, "She saved my life." She wrapped her arms around her distended middle, hugging her unborn baby.

Gage laid Violet on the gurney the EMTs had pulled out. "She took one in the chest." He climbed out and put his arms around his wife.

The medics shoved the gurney inside the ambulance, and one got to work. "We have to go."

Gage turned to him. "Blake, go with them. You, too, Clare."

She nodded and climbed in the back.

"Later, we can talk about what that was." Gage speared his wife with a look.

"I had it handled." But the fear in Clare's eyes was real.

Gage didn't seem so convinced, but the residual fear was probably also coursing through his veins. "Go, Blake."

There was such a mess here.

Lives had been lost. Officers killed in the line of duty. His father had done what Violet seemed to have done as well. Blake's body went cold.

Numb.

"Go." Gage shoved him in the ambulance.

Blake slid onto the bench seat. His heart was shattered. He could barely look while the medic worked on her. No idea what the guy was doing or if Violet would even survive.

Clare reached over and grabbed his hand, holding on.

Blake shut his eyes and leaned his head back against a cabinet. A machine beeped in a rhythm. Steady.

"Is there someone I can call for you?"

What did that mean? He opened his eyes and looked at Clare. "What?"

"Someone who can sit with you. It'll be a long day of waiting."

He said, "Violet has a grandmother. She'll want to know what's happening."

The ambulance turned a corner, and they all swayed with the movement.

Clare shook her head. "I mean someone who can sit with you."

He didn't call people for that. He took care of things himself. He'd have said Jasper at a push, but the guy was busy.

"Family."

Blake had that in SWAT. But he also had his sisters. "Why don't you tell me where Destiny is, and I'll call the rest of the girls?"

"I didn't know that Jasper hadn't told you. We all thought you knew."

And his friend had protected him when he had other things going on. Kept him from being torn apart by personal, work, and family ties.

"She's on a plane right now, somewhere over Canada. The Famous Ones are escorting her home."

"You'll have to explain that since I have no idea who they are."

Clare said, "Allyson, Tina, Amber, Michelle, and Lily. There are more as well. A whole group of them. They're amazing. They have multiple teams that work across the world."

"For Vanguard?"

"I can't talk about what they do. It's all hush-hush, top-secret government contracts. They're the best of the best. Kidnap and ransom, retrieval, rescues. It's all very *Mission: Impossible*, if you can believe it."

"I'll believe it if it means my sister is all right and headed home." Here in Benson, they'd saved his father—before he chose to give his life.

"I'd love to tell you story after story about the Famous Ones and what they do. But if I do that, I'll end up disappearing to one of those secret government prisons I'm not supposed to know about. Probably for the rest of my life. And I don't want to have this baby in one of those places. Gage wouldn't like it."

"No, I don't reckon he would."

She smiled and squeezed his hand.

He listened to the beep of Violet's heart for another few seconds. Then, the ambulance stopped.

Violet was whisked out in a rush of medical staff.

Please be okay. "She'll live, right?" He had to ask. He'd watched the life leave his father's eyes. He didn't know why one person lost their life while another continued.

Clare said, "Keep praying, and don't stop."

After what seemed like forever, he finally spotted his sisters racing into the waiting area. "Blake!"

Hope ran to him first with Mercy right behind her. Grace hung back. But she'd probably driven the others here and was working on holding it together for their sake.

Hope and Mercy slammed into him. He looked at Grace. "Get over here."

Her face crumpled, and she started to cry. They gathered Grace into their huddle.

Blake said, "Destiny will be home soon. She's okay."

Someone sobbed. Maybe it was him.

"Is Lettie going to be okay?" Hope swiped at her cheeks, staring up at him with those huge brown eyes that made him want to give her whatever she wanted. But he had to be strong.

"We're waiting to find out, kid." He kissed her cheek. "What you can do right now is meet Violet's granny." The girls had never had a grandparent before.

He let them go, but Hope snuggled up to his side.

Doris stood, a nervous smile on her face that he didn't expect. "Hello, girls."

Blake said, "This is Hope, that's Grace. And there's Mercy."

Doris's smile widened. "You all have beautiful names. You can call me Granny. That's what Violet calls me."

Mercy sobbed and launched herself at the trim older woman. Doris held on to her. "I know, child. It's scary when you have to wait, but we can pray together."

What about Violet's father? "Granny?"

She looked at him. "Yes, child?"

One of the girls giggled.

"Is there a way we can call George and let him know what happened?" As far as Blake knew the guy had been arrested.

Her expression shuttered. "We should pray for him, too."

"Okay." He nodded.

The girls looked at him.

Blake lifted his hands. "It's new. But I pray now."

Who knew that would make them all burst into tears?

A doctor wandered over. "Violet Anderson's family?"

They huddled together, holding hands.

Granny said, "Yes?"

"She's out of surgery. She's going to be just fine."

FORTY-TWO

Blake opened the door ahead of her and stepped inside.

Violet had regained a lot of her strength. She hadn't returned to work as a paramedic yet since she couldn't pass the physical that had her lifting heavy weights. But she had attended many meetings and orientations for her new job at Vanguard.

It involved some travel, given she needed to be on hand for operations where they considered injury possible.

Since she woke up from the hospital surrounded by her family in the past few weeks, her father had been indicted. The police were still looking for the remnant of the shooters who had opened fire on a crowd of cops. And the person who had ordered the hit.

Even though he had executed the attack, Malik

Henderson was killed in the drive-by shooting outside the funeral. Jamal Reed had also lost his life that day.

Four police officers had died. A handful of cops had been winged. One had medically retired, but most were ready to get back to work.

She'd been released a couple of days after Dennis, and they'd spent a good amount of time talking on video chat. What with both of them recovering from gunshots. They were helping each other stay on track.

Blake had slept on the couch at Granny's since Violet got home. So that she didn't feel unsafe when the memories hit, and probably also for himself. So he didn't feel alone.

He'd had his father cremated, and the girls had gone with him to a mountain hilltop where they'd spread his ashes so he could be free. At peace. They all knew where he would spend eternity.

The pastor from Benson Community Church had come over a few times and even brought his father, the former pastor, with him. More than likely, the old man was sweet on Granny, but she wouldn't give up any details.

"Are you coming?" Blake held out his hand, amusement on his face.

It was all a little too suspicious. "Why was there a dress code for family dinner?"

He smiled wide.

"And why are we at Gage and Clare's house?" The place was gorgeous and slightly huge.

"We have a date."

Violet frowned.

"And you have a job to do." He tugged her inside, then down the hall to the dining room and a set of French doors.

"Okay, I'm confused. What are..."

She got a look at the backyard. "Who is getting married?"

What kind of surprise was this? She and Blake had talked about what dating meant for two believers—it wasn't just a holding pattern or an amusement while it lasted. This was about seeing if they wanted to spend their lives together.

Had he jumped the gun and set something up?

"I am."

Violet spun around, wincing at a lingering ache where the bullet had torn through her. But if not her, then it would've hit Clare, and *no one* would've accepted that. She couldn't have lived knowing she hadn't done everything she could to save an innocent life.

"Granny?" She blinked at Doris, who wore a shimmery ivory-colored dress. "Wait." Her hair had a sleeker style, and her makeup was less everyday glamor and more classic beauty. "You're getting—"

"I did say throwing her for a loop might not be the best plan." Blake folded his arms across his chest. He'd shown up at the townhouse in slacks and a dark purple shirt. She had on the dress she'd bought for her first date with Blake because he'd insisted that she wear it again.

Granny waved a hand. "Come on, dear. You can give me away."

"What?" Violet sputtered.

"I'm marrying Lawrence." She handed Violet the smaller of the two bouquets of flowers she was holding.

"Since when?"

Blake sighed.

Granny shook her head. "Since right now, dear. I'm not getting any younger."

"You're gonna move out? I have to live in the townhouse by myself?"

Granny kissed her cheek. "Hopefully, not for long."

She dragged Violet outside, and the speakers went silent.

Then, music began to play. They walked down the aisle to where an older man stood in a dark gray suit and ivory tie.

Violet gasped. "Lawrence looks so handsome."

Things kind of got blurry, and words swam together.

She was crying.

The fifty people in attendance looked her way. The pastor. Her granny and Lawrence.

Violet hiccupped.

Blake got out of his chair and came to stand behind her, sliding his arms around her waist and laying his chin on her shoulder. He pressed a tissue into her hands and whispered in her ear. "I love you."

What did the Vanguard people in the audience think of their new tough-chick medic bawling because an old woman was getting married?

She settled back into the feel of Blake's arms. The way she had when the fear got the best of her. When she'd realized he needed her because the loss of his father was too close. When the girls came over to watch a movie, there wasn't enough room on the couch, so they had to scoot close to each other. His embrace made her life sweeter.

Destiny had a shadow about her, but she was healing. She didn't say much about what happened and occasionally left the room to take a phone call. They tried to be understanding, but things would come to a head soon enough, and the family would call her on her secrets.

Adding the girls to her life, more so than they'd been in it before, was one thing. But why did Granny marrying Lawrence feel like taking something away? It should feel like adding a grandpa. The guy was nice enough. He made everyone laugh. His coffee could bring a centuries-past dead elephant back to life.

"I want to marry you."

She closed her eyes. It was that or watch Granny kiss her husband.

"On a beach. With you in a bikini."

Violet chuckled silently.

"I'll wear shorts and flip-flops, and you can wear one of those flowers in your hair. And we'll disappear for two weeks afterward and ignore *everything*."

She smiled. "That sounds amazing."

"I love you."

She turned to face him. "I know."

"And we're doing it *soon*." He tugged her even closer.

She smiled. "I can't wait."

He touched his lips to hers and kissed her the way he always did but with an added note of promise. The wedding audience clapped an extra round just for them.

One of the girls yelled, "Now we party!"

ABOUT THE AUTHOR

Find out more about Lisa Phillips at her website, where you can check out her work with Sunrise Publishing and find Lisa on Social Media.
https://authorlisaphillips.com/about-the-author

If you loved this book, please consider sharing about it on social media. Or leave a review at your book retailer website, on Goodreads, or on Bookbub. Your review will help others find great books to entertain and encourage them! For a FREE novel from Lisa Phillips, scan the QR code below to connect to Lisa's newsletter and be the first to hear about sales, new books, and recommendations for your TBR pile.

facebook.com/authorlisaphillips

instagram.com/lisaphillipsbks

bookbub.com/authors/lisa-phillips

ALSO BY LISA PHILLIPS

Find out more about Benson First Responders on the series page:

https://authorlisaphillips.com/benson-first-responders

Benson First Responders is a continuation of Last Chance Downrange. Read the whole Last Chance Downrange series now!

Point of Impact

Hard Target

Hollow Point

Terminal Velocity

Audio Available from Podium Publishing

Find more stories based in Last Chance County at: www.lastchance-county.com

Other series by Lisa:

Brand of Justice (Thriller series)

Benson First Responders (Christian Romantic Suspense)

Last Chance Fire & Rescue (Sunrise Publishing)

Chevalier Protection Specialists

Last Chance County

Northwest Counter-Terrorism Taskforce

Double Down

WITSEC Town (Sanctuary)

And numerous other titles including several from
Love Inspired Suspense.

Find the complete list here:

https://authorlisaphillips.com/full-book-list